A Riot of Red Ribbon

Also in the Gypsy Girl trilogy

The Parsley Parcel

The first of Freya's adventures. Will
her Romany magic be strong enough to
fulfil a promise and grant Emma
Hemmingway's deepest wish?

Gold and Silver Water

Freya is summoned to help Penny, a
girl imprisoned in sadness. Can she
find a way to unlock the healing power
of gold and silver water?

A Riot of Red Ribbon

by Elizabeth Arnold

For Bob, who is my rock and Miriam,
a gently guiding star

First published in Great Britain in 1998
by Mammoth
This TV tie-in edition published 2001
by Mammoth, an imprint of Egmont Books UK
a division of Egmont Holding Limited
239 Kensington High Street, London W8 6SA

Text copyright © 1998 Elizabeth Arnold

Cover photographs by Nigel Dickinson copyright © 2000 Film
and General Productions Ltd

The moral right of the author has been asserted

ISBN 0 7497 4592 4

10 9 8 7 6 5 4 3 2 1

A CIP catalogue record for this title is available from the
British Library

Printed and bound in Great Britain by Cox & Wyman Ltd,
Reading, Berkshire

Contents

The Summons

'Ye shall come through brake and
fen
Ye shall come through thorn or
forest
Ye shall come over hill, down dale.
Ye shall come neither clothed nor
naked
Ye shall come neither walking or
flying
Ye shall come neither in sun nor
moon.
Ye shall come neither anointed or
unanointed
Ye shall come neither in haste nor
sloth.'

Believed to be of medieval origin.

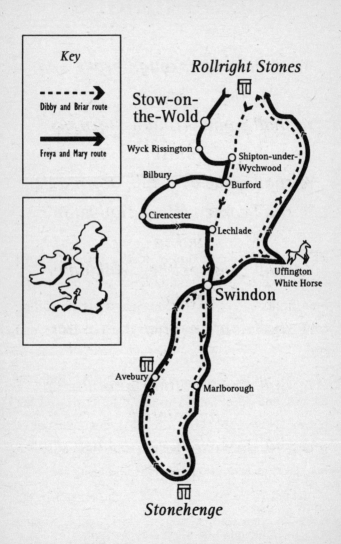

Key

- - - → Dibby and Briar route

——→ Freya and Mary route

Rollright Stones

Stow-on-the-Wold

Wyck Rissington

Shipton-under-Wychwood

Bilbury

Burford

Cirencester

Lechlade

Uffington
White Horse

Swindon

Avebury

Marlborough

Stonehenge

1 The cross-over time

The gnarled finger slowly traced the outline of the distant granites, fringing them with an esoteric blue light that shimmered uneasily, as if waiting for an instruction, a command between finger and stone.

Great-gran, the most patriarchal of Romany queens, had no intention of giving up one jot of her power. Heaven, she'd learned, was what you made of it and, for Great-gran, heaven was the chance to meddle. It was the very thing she did best.

I knew none of this when I found myself in the cross-over time, that moment which is neither waking nor sleeping, living nor dying, that transitory state which seems so pleasant, and yet is the most dangerous of all.

I stood in the middle of Rollright Stones. My stomach was twist-trembly tight, for here, when the blue light dances, truths must be discovered, and rules of place and time become a law unto themselves.

I backed to lean against the tallest stone, pretending all this magic was of no concern to me. I was doing the only thing I could – waiting. For once firelight flickers kiss stone, you may not leave.

The weaving flashes spun bluer and brighter, creating a web of such intensity that I was sucked back into the circle centre. My ears filled with a strange impassioned sound that was neither flute nor violin, pure sweet notes that called to me even though I'd never heard them before. My brain was tingle-tune active, but it wasn't fear I felt, not even when Pahn, the spirit guardian of the night, emerged from the encircling stone and gazed at me with gobble-green eyes.

It wasn't fear that made me shiver-shudder, my eyes not wanting to see, my ears not wanting to acknowledge my calling; it was a growing unease, a feeling that I would never be allowed to be *me*.

The music grew stronger and wilder, tugging my heartstrings until the pain in my chest was more than I could bear.

'Come!' ordered Great-gran, her voice sounding as bossy-boots booming as it had ever been.

I looked to where Great-gran should be, but saw only Pahn, black fur licked by purple flames, green eyes drawing me.

'Where's Great-gran?' I said stubbornly. 'It's Great-gran that commanded me.'

The sleek, black panther rose up on to his hind legs, his lips curled back to reveal strong white fangs.

'Oh, come on, Pahn! I am a chime child, you can't scare *me*.'

The snarl became a smile, the lean and hungry cat a lithesome human stranger. The man and the spirit panther Pahn were somehow one, and I knew they'd been sent in pursuit of me.

'Come!' called the incomer, his green eyes drawing me as much as his strangely compelling music. 'I said *come*.'

'To me!' commanded Great-gran.

'No, to me!' ordered the stranger.

In the outside world I stood alone, yet my string-puppet limbs and aching heart were being ripped between them. I felt confused. I sensed more than mere mischief afoot.

'How can I follow my calling,' I told them crossly, 'when I'm being filleted like a supper-time fish?' I heard the rich chuckle that meant for once Great-gran was listening. The blue lights spluttered and were gone.

My name is Freya Boswell, I mind-muttered as I stood at the very heart of Rollright Stones, my eyes staring unseeing at the freshly ploughed fields that lay empty before me like a sea of soft leather. I am a chime child, so *perfectly* safe. I stand here all alone in the middle of the night, like a loopy lemon, because I have no choice but to come when I am called, but that does not mean I have to be afraid.

'You're up to mischief, Great-gran!' I called to the empty sky.

'Who, me?'

I laughed. Great-gran was never very good at playing the fresh-faced innocent. I felt no panic, not even when the dizzily dancing violet sprites sprung to life again, an augury foretelling the importance of her coming. They grew ever deeper and darker,

4

wilder and closer, so close that they brushed my naked toes.

'It's no good, Great-gran! All the fire in the world can't tumble-tremble mix me.'

'But I can!' Great-gran chuckled. 'You wait and see. Chime Child, there is still much in life you have to experience.'

'What must I learn now?'

There was no answer from the azure-tinged mirage in the muddy earth sea, but, as if in answer, the light lances ringing the rough rocks grew even stronger and braver.

The circle of stones is known as the King's Men, but the tune they danced to then was commanded by *my* great-gran.

I stood rabbit still as the blue lightning capered stormily round my body. Swirling lances slowly fused into a single strike which struck the tallest stone, wakening once more the handsome stranger.

He leaned idly against the ancient rocks, him one side of centre, me the other. He was dressed in black, apart from a scarlet cummerbund. The edges of his trailing belt fluttered gently, even though there seemed not to be a breath of air.

5

'My name is Churen Isaacs and I am summoned to you.'

'And I am drawn to you,' I replied, feeling his melodic voice eat into my heart, producing a yearning so deep I could give it no name.

I stepped forward, reaching out my hand to him, as he reached to me, but as our fingers met the earth went black, and he was gone.

2 'This magic belongs to all of us'

The night had been warm and wet, the new moon dressed in a shining shimmer-haze. I had watched it pass alone, sucking night-time quiet deep into my bones.

Mary, my gorgio friend, was lump-log sleeping. Mary never likes greeting the first mists of morning. Sometimes I wonder why she ever comes to stay with me. She slumber-sleeps for hours, does Mary. Eventually the moment came when I *had* to nudge her into wakefulness. 'Come outside.'

'Freya! It's three in the morning!'

'Shh! Don't wake Briar Rose. Come outside.'

7

'Why?'

'Great-gran commands us, even Dibby.'

'You are no longer a pawn! Great-gran is *dead*, and Dibby is . . . dibby'

'So?'

Mary scowled, dragged on her dressing-gown, rooted about for her slippers and hissed, all at the same time, 'I'm fed up with your stupid magic, Freya.'

'It's not *my* magic,' I told her. 'This magic belongs to all of us.'

Mary was still scowling as she followed me the short distance from our vardo to the circle. We wandered together round the ancient granites, mostly because it made Mary feel less silly than just standing.

'Just why do we keep having to visit this heap of old rocks?' Mary asked, nudging one with her foot. 'Especially now.'

'Because they are here, and the world is sleeping.'

'So what?'

'Doesn't their power gnaw into your bones?'

'No,' Mary said, inspecting the mud on her slipper, 'they don't seem that special to me. They just look like lumpy rocks being slowly eaten away by lichens and mosses.'

8

'Time is here.'

'And flying pigs.'

'Listen, Mary, we have been drawn to things that were here before, and will be soon. Can't you see?'

'No.'

'Well, Dibby does!' I said crossly. 'Dibby knows she can never be really lonely while the stones are her friends. Great-gran told her so – and Dibby's birthday is tomorrow, so we have come.'

Mary thought I was screw-loose simple and I couldn't blame her: Great-gran *was* dust-ash dead; Dibby had a grown-up body and a small-child mind; it was the middle of the night and raining.

Mary opened her mouth . . .

'Shh!'

On the far side of the stone circle, just within its boundaries, Dibby stood alone, her arms spread out, as if unaware of the tender rain. She gazed towards a distant group of granites called the Whispering Giants.

'Shall we fetch her back?'

I shook my head. 'Things within the circle must be left to happen.'

'Even if they are daft?' Mary said, watching a black cat with a red collar emerge from the small wood of pines, stroll to the centre of the circle and brush its body gently against Dibby's legs.

I grinned, 'Yes, even if they are daft.'

Beyond the cordon of rocks, night-black pines whispered, as if conferring with the distant stone knights. Dibby stared out across the hills, showing not the least sign of morning-damp cold.

The strange black cat gave up seeking attention. It lifted its tail high and strutted back to the shelter of the fluttering trees.

'Odd Dibby took no notice,' Mary sounded puzzled. 'She likes cats.'

'That was no ordinary cat. It was Bastet, the Egyptian goddess of joy,' I told Mary. 'Dibby is sad, she feels lonely, she is so miserable deep inside that she doesn't see her. Life's not easy when you have a wheel-dented brain.'

'How can she be lonely among the stones which Great-gran said are her friends?' Mary replied, sounding screw-mouth, acid-tongued.

'Would you like it if the only things that really seemed to understand you were stones?'

'Well, I'm sure they're the only things that understand *you*!' Mary snorted, adding, 'Look!'

A brightly coloured wagon drove across the freshly ploughed field on the far side of the stone circle. It was a green and gold Reading wagon, but as radiantly painted as my own. An ebony Shire horse pulled it easily over the freshly ridged earth, stopping just outside the perimeter.

Churen Isaacs climbed nonchalantly down and strolled towards Dibby Gran. His pace easy, his footstep light.

'Well, he's a very early visitor,' Mary whispered, her eyes suddenly butter bright with interest. 'Do you know him?'

'We've met once,' I told her truthfully, watching the long, red silks of his belt flow sensuously with the fine movements of his body.

'Isn't he wonderful!' Mary breathed, and the sun peeped more boldly over the horizon as if wanting to give us a better view.

'I think he's a little chancy,' I told Mary, not liking the strength of her stare.

'Oh, Freya!' Mary replied, gently pushing me. 'Sometimes you can be so silly!'

I turned to face my gorgio friend, and when I looked back the incomer and the vardo were gone.

Dibby stood just as before, staring silently into the dawn-kissed mists.

'It's got to be somewhere,' Mary said. '*He's* got to be somewhere.'

I shrugged. Mary is stamp-foot stubborn, so there would be no peace until she was sure. We searched the fields in the first light of dawn. As I expected, we found no sign of the great Shire, nor of the brightly painted wagon. In a muddy rut rested a scrap of red ribbon. I stuffed it into my pocket while Mary searched the gently rolling field.

'No ruts and no horse droppings,' Mary said in amazement.

'And no noise,' I told her. 'Didn't you think it a little bit odd that there was no noise?'

Mary stomped over to Dibby. 'You must have seen him!' she said, poking Dibby to make sure she was listening. Dibby Gran shook her head. 'He was right in front of your nose,' Mary insisted. 'Come on, Dibby, where did he go?'

'He was never here,' Dibby said through chattering teeth, her thin nightdress giving her no protection from the gentle rain.

'So why are you?' Mary asked crossly.

Dibby Gran stared at Mary, as if *she* was the one who was skull-rattle senseless. 'Because I was called too, silly!' she said. 'Great-gran has a plan. I know she has, she told me!'

3   Rollright Stones

'Who's coming to this party?'

'Everyone.'

'Everyone?' asked Mary. 'Who's everyone?'

'My brothers, including Tashar and Vashti.' Tashar is my best brother, and the one who makes my shoes. Vashti is the messiest, but he can make a violin sing. 'All the Romanies in the area, even Kokko George, we sort of share that poshrat, don't we?'

Mary laughed. 'I never knew he was part Romany until you came.'

'And he never spoke of you, not even when the drúkkerébema that led me to Aunt Emma was arranged. That prophesy was so hard to fulfil, Mary.'

'I know, but I'm so glad that we met,' Mary said, offering me a hug-heart smile. I pushed her, to show it wasn't me with the jelly-soft inside.

'Mum and Aunt Emma had babies.'

'Your mam is always having babies!'

'No, I think she's stopped now.' Not surprisingly, Mary sounded pleased. After all, they did have so many.

As we shared our memories we divided a pile of bright wooden beads into piles and offered them round. My best brother Tashar had made them one long, cold winter. We called them baby-boredom blocks. They were the only toys we owned. We had a teddy once, but that was long ago.

'Is Emma's Briar a proper gorgio?' Mary asked, remembering my very first magic.

'Are you a proper gorgio?' I teased, thinking of Kokko George.

'Of *course* I am!' Mary retorted, her voice stamp-stubborn sure, but her dancing fingers flickered doubts.

We were busy minding the youngest children while Mam was nagging the reluctant Roms into helping the women with party preparations. The men wouldn't have anything to do with the food, except for fetching and carrying sacks, but they were happy to make sure that the log piles and the drink stacks were almost sky high, wagons neatly parked and chickens, dogs and horses properly fed and watered.

'I can't believe that Aunt Emma let Briar Rose come.'

'She's expecting the twins soon, and she's moving house, and Briar Rose is a lovely, lively lump,' I told Mary, smiling as I watched Briar making the brightest necklace of all.

'Even so . . .'

'Don't eat the beads!' I warned the tiny chavo sitting next to Briar. 'Let me thread them for you.'

'Can I stay up late?' piped up little Briar Rose. 'Can I stay up late too?'

'Aunt Emma won't like it,' Mary warned.

'Aunt Emma won't *know*,' I told her, grinning at Briar, who could nag as well as Mary and I, even though she was pint-pot small.

'I'm Romany born, so it's my party too.'

'You're not Romany born,' Mary told Briar. 'You're even more gorgio than me.'

'I'm a magic Romany,' Briar Rose said confidently, 'like Freya.'

'God forbid, two of them!' Mary screeched,

throwing her hands up in the air and raising her eyes to heaven.

I had to laugh, and so did Briar Rose. We collapsed into a giggle-heap, making Mary out-face scowly.

'Ah, but think,' I told Mary, not wanting her to feel left out, 'you *do* have more Romany blood than Briar. Your blood line runs from Kokko George, and no matter how much Great-gran muttered and scowled when he married out, she was always deep-heart fond of the poshrat George.

'So, can I stay up all night?' Briar asked eagerly. 'Just like you?'

'This is a Romany festa,' I warned Briar. 'Just don't tell Aunt Emma and Uncle Jack *anything* when you get home. They will only wobble-worry. You can stay up until the sandman steals you, but only if you button your lip. This party will not be the least bit like having tea on the lawn.'

'I won't tell Mum and Dad,' Briar agreed. 'Promise.'

'It's such a small world,' Mary said thoughtfully, as she offered Briar Rose a buni manridi, which is what we Romanies call honey cake. 'When we met, I never dreamed we could be related.'

'Kokko George is not a *proper* Romany,' I reminded Mary firmly. 'He's a didakai. His dad broke the rules and married out.'

'Am I a proper Romany?' Briar Rose quizzed, her ears more active than her fingers.

'No! Well . . . only the magic bit.'

'So do I belong?'

'Yes,' Mary said kindly. 'Briar Rose, you are like Kokko George, linked to both of us.'

'Why on earth does Dibby want her party here?' asked Mary as we all dressed up for the evening. 'The stones might be her friends but . . .'

'I told you! Rollright is her birth circle, the place where she is closest to both the earth and the sky. Mostly poor old Dibbs feels outside-odd. *Everyone* tries to protect her, but all she wants is to be treated just the same.

'So she's lonely?'

'Dibbs says she never feels lonely here, she says the stones are her special friends, but she *is*. Poor Dibby is too childish to want to play with Mam, and too grown-up to be totally happy with Briar. She's sort of lost between worlds.'

'But everyone adores her.'

'I know,' I said sadly, 'but we don't know how to let her grow. We can never get into her mind, we can never quite see the world in the colours she paints.'

'Well, she'll be happy tonight,' Mary said, frowning as I chose a skirt of swirling scarlet. 'I recognise that colour! Nothing to do with Churen Isaacs, is it?'

I laughed and tried to act all casual. Sometimes Mary was smack-mouth smart. 'Of course not!' I told her firmly. 'You know this is my favourite colour.'

'Well, I think you fancy him.'

'And I think you're stupid.'

We pushed each other to show we were still friends. 'Do you fancy him?' I asked.

'Of course not,' Mary said stiffly. 'Now, tell me about this party. Will Vashti play his violin for us?'

I laughed as I picked out my gold sovereign earrings, the ones that Great-gran had left me hidden, as if forgotten, in the depths of the vardo. Great-gran never fooled me. Those earrings were no more lost than the vardo was properly burned. They were not even a memento; no, they were a statement, an assertion that the links between us will always be.

'Oh yes, Vashti will kel the bosh, so don't wear

those shoes!' I told Mary, who looked pale and pretty in summer-sky blue. 'You won't be able to dance for hours in them.'

By the time the party started, gypsies had appeared from everywhere. The fields were full of brightly painted wagons and large shiny caravans, intermixed with big tents, small benders, vans, carts and lorries. Men, women and children were all full-feather dressed and wonderfully bright.

The woods echoed with laughter long before the party began. A huge cooking fire glowed lively. The most amazing foods bubbled gently in suspended pans. Fresh bread and baked potatoes warmed in outside embers. The smells were tummy-rumble exciting. Everyone had contributed something, even Dibby, who had helped the children deck the stones with festa flowers.

Usually, it would be the honoured aged who were greeted first, but everybody knew that Dibby was a simple, shining star and that for her, the rules were dear-heart different.

'How's the birthday girl, then?'

'Well Dibbs, that is a beautiful dress, did you help Mam to sew it? Those stitches are ever so small.'

'Come, Dibbs, you look wonderful. This dance just has to be with me.'

Dibby was wedding-day radiant, her face shining with pride. Her party *was* wild, and just as it should be. Everybody joined in the dancing, there were no wilting lilies here. The stones were filled with vibrant, spinning clothes and hoots of happy laughter. Sometimes the pace of the music was so fast and our skirts swirled so madly, we seemed to be all legs as we danced and clapped to the violin's resonant rhythms. When we tired, Vashti played something moody and slow, and we drifted gently round the ring of garlanded stones like bright butterflies trapped in a ring of light, offering up to them the joy in our hearts.

Hour after hour we danced and sang, until our feet ached and our throats felt dry. We had no sense of time at all. Towards morning some of the oldies crept off to bed, but the rest of us continued to dance until long after dawn.

Sometimes the men stopped to chat and swill beer. Most women quaffed wine, some even fresh, cool water. It didn't matter, there was certainly no Aunt Emma to insist on lemonade. We each chose for

21

ourself, even Briar, who tucked into raspberry fizz like there was no tomorrow.

Many had come to make music. Accordions and simple flutes mixed with fiddles, but always Vashti led, the pure sounds of his violin still rising sweetly hours after we greeted the rising sun.

We were some of us motto, but nobody got cross, nobody spoiled things; it was a special party, and with Romanies you are supposed to be sensible. No one got out of their skull; no one was sick.

I grabbed another buni manridi and glanced towards my vardo. To my surprise I could see Great-gran as clear as day, rocking quietly in her watch-the-world chair. She was smoking her little clay pipe and smiling down on us, as she always did when we danced to her tune.

'I must be going mad,' I muttered to Mary. 'I can see Great-gran up in my vardo . . . *her* vardo, keeping her beady eye on us.'

'Ye gods!' Mary said. 'I can see her too.'

We waved in delight. It was right that Great-gran should come to Dibby's party. Great-gran puffed smoke rings into the air and waved back. We laughed. We were still giggling as she disappeared from view.

Oh yes, Dibby had wanted a party, a wild, stone-circle party, and that was exactly what happened. It was only when we woke later in the morning that we remembered that seeing Great-gran laugh almost always meant trouble.

4 'Listen! Dibby and Briar have run away!'

I felt like I had just crashed into sleep when I was shaken like a cloth-wrapped salad. 'Freya! Wake up! Dibby Gran, Briar Rose, the horse Bryony *and* your precious vardo, they're all missing!'

I scrambled to shake the sleepy dust from my eyes. We young ones had slept heavy-head easy, curled up in little groups where we had chattered ourselves to sleep. Dibby had been there then, and Briar.

'Come *on*, Freya. Aunt Emma will go mad when she hears. Where can they have gone? Freya, listen! Dibby and Briar have *run away*!'

'They'll be close,' I said, trying to sound more reassuring than I felt. 'I expect Dibby's moved the vardo further from the camp, so Briar could feather-down sleep in a bit of quiet.'

'She's not *anywhere*,' Mary screeched, finally managing to shake my sleepy brain into worry-wakefulness. 'I've looked! I'll get the blame for this. Aunt Emma said I was to make sure you took good care of her. She will be all right, Freya? Tell me she will?'

'You've looked? Already?'

Mary glared at me. 'Did you expect me to sleep on that cold, hard earth for hours like you do? Anyway, some funny music woke me, so I've searched everywhere. The only thing I saw was that stupid black cat.'

'Funny music?' I asked, my muddle-mindedness totally gone. 'What sort of funny music?'

'I don't know!' Mary snapped. 'It's not important. Now are *you* going to tell your mother or am I?'

We searched the camp, the fields, the village. Nobody had noticed my lovely old wagon, not mixed up among so many. Nobody had seen Briar or Dibby at all.

We gathered round the lunch-time fire. Everyone was worried. Dibby had never taken it into her head to disappear before.

'Aunt Emma will go frantic when I tell her,' Mam muttered, wiping a tear that had crept unbidden into her eye. 'I don't think she was really happy with Briar staying so long anyway . . . and Dibbs, poor Dibbs.'

'You mustn't worry! Mary and I have four whole weeks to find them.'

'Aunt Emma and Uncle Jack are expecting you to write . . . and Briar.'

'We'll send postcards,' I promised. 'I can write like Briar, she's only clench-first-and-grab small, so anybody can.'

'What shall I say if anybody asks for her?' Mam asked, screwing her cooking apron into a muddled rag ball.

I felt sorry for my mam. Usually it was her giving orders now Great-gran was gone. She must have been deep-heart scared to listen so quiet.

'For goodness sake Mam, just act all calm like you do when the gavvers come poky-nose prying . . .'

'Gavvers?'

'Policemen, Mary, surely you know that! If you have to, tell Aunt Sally we've gone on a walkabout with Kokko George. She doesn't see him in summer, anyway, he's too busy making wicker things for tourists. She'll tell Aunt Emma, and everyone will think we're perfectly safe.'

'Dibby will have left patterans,' Vashti said as he rose to leave. 'They'll soon be found. Dibby's trail signs are always brightly coloured.'

'Nobody would harm them,' Tashar added, giving Mam a reassuring hug. 'Not a dibby lady and a dot of a child, and I'll bet they've not gone far.'

'We'll find them.'

'You'll not have to worry.'

'Someone will bring them back.'

Slowly, families split up to leave, promising not to stop searching until Dibby and Briar were found.

Mary and I checked hospitals, no gypsies had been seen at all, then we visited police stations. I have never ever hobnobbed with so many gavvers, but I have to say they were very kind. I had to tell a few small lies, though: I pretended that Briar was a Romany, I said she was six, not four, and I didn't let on that her gorgio name was Rose. I dare not let Aunt

27

Emma hear a worry whisper, not until Briar was safely found.

'Why has she gone?' Mam asked again and again as the day dripped slowly by. 'Freya, tell me *why*?'

'Great-gran must have a reason.'

I could give no other explanation, even a chime child needs time to find answers. I just had this feeling that Dibby's disappearance was something to do with music, and something to do with stones.

5 Through the linking crystal

'I'll have to leave the magpie,' I told Mary as we fetched the horses, Elsha and Domino. 'Bastet could show up, and Maggie's fluff-feather scared of cats.'

'Oh, isn't that sad!' Mary smirked. 'No magpie to squawk in your ear or make a mess on your shoulder. It could be fun finding Briar after all.'

'Maggie's my friend!'

'That's *your* problem Freya. I'm your friend too, but that doesn't mean we have to share everything.'

'I'll look after the magpie,' Mam said a bit too reluctantly to please me. 'You take the crystal, Freya.'

'But I don't need it, Mam.'

'I need you to have the crystal, and so does Mary.

29

Anyway, it might be more helpful than you think.'

'Great-gran said we are the guardians. She told me only the Boswell women should know that things can be seen in it.'

'Oh, thanks a lot, Freya!' Mary said huffily. 'I don't want to play with your stupid crystal anyway.'

I gave Mary a gorgio hug. 'Mary, you are my closest friend. If I showed the crystal to anybody it would be you, but Great-gran . . .'

'Great-gran was a stubborn old ostrich,' Mam said, holding out the soft bag that kept our family linking-crystal safe. 'Now she is dead and it is me who decides, and I say that Mary can use the crystal.'

'Are you sure?' I asked, still mindful of huffy Great-gran and her bossy-boot ways.

'I told you . . .' Mary said, but we both ignored her.

'Freya, I would give anyone the crystal, gypsy or gorgio, if I thought they could fetch back Briar Rose and your dibby gran.'

I took the crystal. My mam was weary-eye worried, and the crystal was hers to use as she pleased.

'Anyway,' Mam reminded me, 'the crystal will only work when it knows the holder should see.'

I felt sheepish. My mam was right. I was so used to absorbing its magic, that I had quite forgotten.

'Will I see?' Mary asked, curious in spite of herself. 'What will I see?'

'That is for the crystal to decide, Mary,' Mam said firmly. 'But I'm sure you'll see something. Now go.'

I watched my mam, all open-mouth gaping. Once, it had been *her* pleading for me to stay, and Great-gran who insisted I should leave, and that time too it had been for the sake of Briar Rose.

'Go!' Mam ordered, but it wasn't her face I saw. I was looking straight into the eyes of my crinkle-wrinkle, bossy great-gran. It was Ostrich Gran who was commanding me, of that there wasn't the slightest shadow of doubt.

'We'll find them, Great-gran.'

'I'm sorry, Freya, I didn't mean to boss you like Ostrich, it's just I am so afraid. Briar Rose and Dibbs . . . two children off together.'

'We'll find them, Mam,' Mary said. She was used to us now, and never said Mrs Boswell at all.

'Of course you will,' Mam replied, smiling for the first time for ages. 'The crystal will make sure of that.'

31

'How does the crystal work?'

I shrugged. 'Nobody really knows. It looks shiny as a diamond but it's quartz, and quartz is known for healing. There is quartz in the stones too, very tiny bits that you can't really see. That's why the crystal works even better by stones, sort of like radio. This linking stone is extra special. It has super-sucked into its heart all the love in our family since time began. Some say Urania Boswell used it, and she was a really famous gypsy who lived at the same time as Queen Victoria.'

'Would it work for me if I was all by myself?'

'Only if you grew whole-heart Romany. Only if you learned to relax and tingle-tune your mind.'

I wrapped the linking crystal safely up in a soft, black cloth and tucked it into my carry bag. Mam watched us every moment until we were quite out of sight. She didn't blow simper-soft kisses, she didn't even wave, but we knew she would not be happy until we were all back. Mam is like that, solid and sensible and safe.

'Can we look at the crystal now?' Mary asked, poky-nose curious as soon as we were out of sight.

'No,' I said, making sure our bender was safely

strapped on the piebald cob, Domino, and the cooking stuff on Elsha, the old, grey mare.

'Why?'

'You can only use the crystal when there is a need.'

'We *need* to find Briar and Dibby Gran.'

'Yes, but we don't need the crystal yet.'

'Why?'

'Because Dibby didn't leave a patteran, but Briar did.'

'Briar left trail signs?'

I grinned. 'Briar might be toddle-foot tall but she's wise-owl smart. Briar thought she should be found, so she's left us a trail of brightly coloured beads.

We rode steadily all day. Mary, not used to horses, soon tired, and as soon as she was snuggle-head sleeping, I unwrapped the crystal.

I held it firmly in my hands until it grew warm. Normally, because I am a chime child, born on Good Friday as the clock struck twelve, I have no need of the crystal, but this time my mam was right, it would help me to *see*.

'Write your name, Briar,' I commanded. 'Feel my love, feel you are safe with Dibbs, and write your name for me.'

Briar was safe in my vardo with Dibby Gran. I could see her clearly as I looked into the crystal, which glowed amber from the heat of my hands.

'Can I have a pen please, Dibbs?'

'You want to draw?' Dibby asked, smiling at Briar who shook her head.

'I want to write.'

'You can write?' Dibby asked, her face drop-mouth gaping. 'I'm grown-up and I can't write.'

'Dad taught me. He says I'm a real clever clogs, but I think it's because he's good at teaching. He taught Freya to write too.' Briar gave Dibby a huge hug-me smile. 'I can't cook though, Dibby. My mum won't let me near a saucepan. She says they're far too dangerous, and I'm not allowed near a fire.'

'I can cook,' Dibby said, smiling again. 'Everyone knows I make the best sastra pot in the whole wide world – that is a stew, Briar – and I can light a fire, but not when Mam's there. She says it's dangerous too.'

'Now can I have a pen please, Dibby?'

'I haven't a pen. There isn't one anywhere.' Dibby

looked anxious. 'I'm sorry, Briar, I can't find a pen.'

I shut my eyes and willed myself into Dibby's child-like brain. '*Make one*, Dibbs.'

Dibby frowned as she hunted through the little cupboard drawers. 'I can't find a pen,' she muttered. 'I really can't find a pen.'

'Make a pen, Dibbs,' I willed her. 'It will be fun.'

'Maybe we could use something else,' Dibby told Briar. 'Can you think of anything?' Briar Rose shook her head.

'I want to write for Freya. *Please*, it's important.'

'Burn a stick, Dibbs,' I said, holding the crystal tight so it could better help me to reach her. 'Take a stick from the cooking fire, Dibbs, but make sure it's cold before you do.'

Dibby put her hands to her head and frowned.

'Head hurt?' asked Briar.

'No, thinking,' Dibbs replied, 'just thinking.'

Briar played with the back of an old letter from Mary while she waited. I smiled to myself. Good old Mary always seemed to help make things work, and it couldn't *always* be chance.

Dibbs walked over to the fire where her sastra pot was merrily stewing. Briar Rose followed close behind her. 'Not too near!' Dibby warned, her voice sounding echo-close to Mam's.

'Fire hot,' Briar said mechanically, and waited patiently while Dibbs poked about with a fresh piece of wood. Eventually, Dibby found what she was looking for: a sliver of wood burned slowly black among the ashes. She fished it out towards the edge and waited quietly until she was sure it was cool.

'This'll do.'

'What's that?' asked Briar.

Dibby frowned and shook her head. 'Can't remember, Chime showed me once.'

'Chime?'

Dibby smiled. 'Chime is our wagon name for Freya. It's like your mum calls you Busy Briar sometimes, and like Great-gran was called Ostrich.'

'Why?'

'I don't know,' Dibby answered, handing Briar the blackened stick. 'Does it matter?'

Briar shrugged and took the twig. She looked puzzled. Dibby showed Briar her blackened fingers. 'It writes. Freya showed me once.'

'Like chalk?'

'Yes,' Dibby Gran said, clapping her hands in delight, 'like chalk.'

Briar Rose marched back indoors, carefully holding the charcoal stick in her podgy hand. She leaned her elbow on the top of the cupboard that also served as a chair, spreading out Mary's letter face down. Her face was furrowed in concentration as she wrote carefully on the back.

She took a long time, because she was, after all, only four. Halfway through, Dibby had to go back to the fire and find another stick. The first one had broken from being gripped so hard.

Briar Rose poked her tongue through her teeth and did her very best writing:

Dear Freya,
I am hapy,
Love rose,
xxx
tell Mummy and
daddy

Briar's face shone with pride as she inspected her work. 'We must get the letter to Freya,' she told Dibby.

Dibby Gran scratched her head, not liking to admit that she didn't know how. After a moment she smiled. 'We'll leave a flower patteran,' she said. 'Kokko George will find it. Yes, that's it, the poshrat can deliver your letter.'

As soon as I had copied the shapes of Briar's letters, I tucked them, and the crystal, away. Briar had been happy with Dibby's answer, and I could now send a postcard from her to her mum and dad (Aunt Emma and Uncle Jack to Mary and me). They might be gorgio strict, but it was only because they were fizzle-burst fond of Briar.

I was all misty-muddle-minded. Dibby was roaming the country roads all alone except for Briar. Briar's mum and dad would flip with fury if they ever found out, but Great-gran had assured me that things were exactly as they should be.

I longed to share my worries with Mary. I hated lying to her, really I did, but I knew if I didn't stay zip-mouth silent, I would be soft-suet shredded to nothing by the tongue of my dead great-gran.

On top of all that, the man Churen and the spirit panther Pahn, were somehow haunting me, hunting me down in dreams and in my day-think mind. They made my limbs shiver-shake and my heart tremble. I had never felt that way before. No matter how much I struggled to understand, nothing made sense at all. It was a long time before I crawled into our bender to try to wrap myself in sleep.

6 'Churen Isaacs was fast becoming trouble'

'Where are we going?' Mary asked, bright as a button the following morning.

I was going to mind-think some magic to tease, but then I remembered Churen, the incomer. There was magic enough that was tingle-skin close. I'm not sure,' I told Mary, 'but I think we'll end up at Stonehenge.'

'Why would Dibby want to go to Stonehenge?'

'She has no choice. Sooner or later she will go

there. She has been called by the stones.'

'I hate stones,' Mary said, saddling up Elsha just like I had shown her. 'Your stupid stones cause nothing but trouble, and they don't even *do* anything. The trouble is all deep in your superstitious little minds.'

'Churen Isaacs likes them,' I told her, watching her face full carefully as I spoke.

'Oh! You're looking for *him*, not Dibby,' Mary said. She was trying to trouble tease, but the look in her eye was wrong.

'Do you want to see what Dibby and Briar are doing?' I asked, to make peace. Churen Isaacs was fast becoming trouble. He was like a lodestone; he had magneted both of us, and that wasn't fair, for Mary has always been my closest friend, and now she could steal him when he was intended for me.

'You mean I can look through the crystal at last?'

'Of course,' I said, loving and hating her.

Mary was all eager excited as we tied the horses to a fence and sat ourselves down on the damp-bottom bank. The morning was slow to clear and still pink-mist magical, but Mary made no note of it. She took the crystal as if it was dandelion-feather fragile, rested

41

it carefully on her lap and stared fix-eye deeply into its murky depths.

'It's clearing. I can see them!'

'Then Mam is right, it was meant for you to see.'

Through the crystal we watched Dibby and Briar Rose skipping hand in hand along the country lanes.

'Where are they heading?'

'Chipping Norton, I think.'

'Where's that?' Mary asked, not knowing these parts.

'South,' I said vaguely. 'Now, do you want to watch or not?'

The truly faithful Bryony was plodding along the road behind the laughing girls. If Dibby skipped for ever, then Bryony would follow. If Domino had been harnessed to the vardo instead then anything could have happened, for his is a restless spirit.

'Where are we going?' Briar asked Dibby, skipping so hard that Dibby had to run to catch up.'

'On a journey. That's what gypsies do. I thought we were grown-up enough to travel alone. I thought you should try living free.'

Briar giggled, and slowed down to let her new friend keep pace. 'But why did we have to sneak away, Dibbs?'

'It's Mam. She worries, and I wanted to show you things . . . all by myself. Are you scared?' Dibby frowned. 'Briar, you're not scared, are you?'

'No,' Briar told her calmly, 'not scared. I like a . . .' she struggled to find a word that was almost bigger than she was '. . . a venture,' she said proudly. 'And I think I like the pink fog and being allowed to get up when I wake, and not having to go back to bed at half past seven. I especially like getting my toes wet in the grass.'

Dibby chuckled, and turned her head to look at Briar. As she did she slipped on a poky-nosed stone. Her body just crumbled up like a heap of old jumble.

Mary gasped and let go of the crystal. It rolled down the folds of her skirt towards the rough-surfaced road. I grabbed it before it could sliver-shatter all our memories and all our tomorrows.

'What about Dibby!'

'If you break the crystal, we'll never see!'

I stood in the middle of the road peering into the crystal. Mary grabbed me and pulled me back on to the bank.

'We don't want two accidents, do we?'

Together, we saw that Briar Rose was still staring

43

in horror at Dibby Gran. 'Are you poorly?'

Slowly, Dibby Gran unfolded herself and gazed up at Briar. Her face was gravel-graze red, her knee was cut and bleeding, but it was her eyes that were saddest of all. 'It wasn't me that should have fallen, I'm grown up!'

'It was the stone,' Briar told Dibby firmly as she tried to pull her up. 'It was a big stone, a nasty stone tripped you up.'

Dibby sniffed and tried to wipe her face with a grubby hand. Briar wetted her handkerchief with her tongue and dabbed at Dibby Gran's knees.

Mary and I watched my grandmother stand like the small child she really was, allowing herself to be lick-hanky rubbed and cleaned, and magic-kissed better. 'I'm the grown-up,' she muttered, but she still let Briar pull her down so she could gently clean her bruised and bleeding cheek. '*I'm* supposed to be the grown-up!'

Briar Rose stopped her rubbing, dropped her bottom lip and stared dolefully at Dibby Gran. 'I'm hungry, Dibbs, very hungry. Can we have some breakfast, please?'

Dibby forgot about her cut knee; she stopped

caring about her stinging face; she was sunshine smiling again.

'Are you hungry, precious angel?'

Briar nodded. Dibby gently took her hand and led her back to the vardo. 'We shall have breakfast at once,' Dibby said, smiling broadly. 'You will be quite safe on this journey. I will always take care of you Briar Rose, you should know that.'

7   Through the maze

By the time Mary and I reached Wyck Rissington on the edge of Stow-on-the-Wold, she was wobble-bone weary. I set up the bender in the fields close to the village green, made her a quick supper, and left her to sleep.

I was happy to be camping here. Wyck is one of the places where our roots are old-time ancient. We even have our own part of the churchyard. Most of us get bone-buried in God-holy ground now . . . It's like an extra insurance, my mam says.

This dead bone place is mostly for Loveridge clans. I could be buried here, for Kokko George has some Loveridge blood, and he is related to both me and Mary, so her bones could lie here too, if she took to our Romany ways. My great-gran talked once of a Loveridge boy jumping the broomstick with an Isaacs. If I was hop-heart hopeful I could believe it was Churen's mam, or his great-gran, or some long-time relative back, so this would be his place too . . . If I was loopy love-sick, I could imagine him close to me . . . but I'm not like that . . . am I?

I still felt a bit gut-tremble guilty because Dibby and Briar were making camp west of Wychwood Forest and we were miles away. It was not that I was being tetchy-toe difficult about fetching her back. I wanted to obey my mam, but Great-gran had commanded me. She had returned from the happy place, where she should be resting for ever, to give me the best of her bossy-boot ways.

So that was how I found myself alone in the churchyard at close to midnight, staring at a cross made from living yew. 'Not here,' Great-gran's voice rang clear in my head. 'Walk on.'

I wandered round to the left of the little churchyard and found myself staring at our Romany graves. The Loveridge family had frothy-foamed their dead with freshly picked flowers. I waited patiently for the clouds to undress the moon so I could see the words carved from the stone. They might have *of no fixed abode* carved on the headstone, but they certainly were not forgotten.

'They are mostly Loveridge graves,' I shouted up to Great-gran. 'Closer to the poshrat than me. There's a Stanley and a Cakebread too, but what is this to me now? Dying is not on my list of things I want to do!'

'*You* should know that every Romany grave is special,' Great-gran retorted, 'as is every Romany. Now, I have plans for you, so go through the maze.'

I've long ago given up trying to ignore Ostrich Gran. It always means trouble. I held my head Romany high, even though I was tremble-toe scared of such a lonely walk on gorgio-God holy ground. Reluctantly I entered the whispering willow maze that stood in the vicarage garden to the left of the church, and tried to pretend that I didn't care that the willows whispered eerily as they closed tight behind me.

Once, long ago, a vicar called Harry Cheales had had a dream. His God, who was as bossy as my great-gran, had commanded him to build a maze of willow.

At the heart of the maze stood a single sequoia tree which represented the tree of heaven.

I knew all of this, but I still felt fizzy fearful as I walked through the waving, night-shadow willows with only the moon to care for me.

At certain places along the maze path hung wooden tablets delicately carved with little figures. I wished Mary was with me and not soaked in sleep. She knew about churches, she understood the mysteries. She was not Jesus-muddle minded like me.

The Reverend Cheales had built his maze to represent the path of life, child to adult, adult to angel, a natural progression, but I felt I was being herded, not walking free. Dibby must feel like this, always being pulled and pushed into the things she must do, and the person mam thinks she must be. I wondered if we all danced like puppets in the game of life, and if so, who pulled the strings? I imagined it could be the gorgio gods, or the misty music that meant Churen was about to tear our heart thinks into slither shreds, or the poky-plotting fingers that had not lost their power even when Great-gran was dust-ash burned.

By one plaque, with the writing *XIV*, there was a sign that read:

LIFE AFTER DEATH

If you don't believe it turn back

The sign was no problem for me. Life after death was clear enough. There was, after all, no escape from my bossy-boots great-gran.

My feet did not want to go on, they were frozen in fear. The next bit of the path was cloaked in total darkness. To a Gorgio, this showed that it was supposed to be like the tunnel of death. My great-gran thought that was a rubbish idea! She's told me since I was toddle-foot small about the morning star that gathers you up when you take your final sleep on the sweet-smelling earth.

I didn't like the tunnel of death. The willows were densely planted and mixed with night-black fir. Even the moon hid. I was so scared my lips stayed glue-stuck sealed, even when Pahn emerged from the darkness and gazed at me with saucer-green eyes. 'Pahn does not mean death,' I told myself so I could stay knight-armour brave. 'He is the night hunter, and if I was supposed to be a meal I would already be chomped-up-stew food.'

Pahn came closer. Still the only thing I could see was his eyes. They glowed like green lanterns. I stood fixed like a heart-stopped rabbit. Not even my breath dared move.

Pahn brushed round my legs as if he was Bastet bringing joy. His fur felt soft, his body warm. I stopped being a sicky-scared baby and let him lead me into the darkness. I rested my hand on his back for comfort. His body felt soft and warm, his scent somehow familiar. I was just beginning to like him when moonlight lit up the way out from the tunnel of death. Pahn hissed softly, a strange noise, half snake, half roar. I bent to thank him but he was already gone.

Now I was free to tread the stepping-stones that showed the way to the happy-place life. Soon there was another gate, with a sign that read:

GATE OF JUDGEMENT
No turning back

I had no idea what it meant. The only person who judged me was Great-gran. She was the one who had patiently made me into a choviar; she was the one who had best grasp of my strings. I wondered if she would ever believe that I had grown up enough to walk life's path all alone.

As I walked though the judgement gate towards the central sequoia, the clock struck twelve. I knew at once that chance did not walk with me.

It was Churen Isaacs, not Great-gran, who waited. He leaned idly against the trunk of the ancient tree. 'I knew you would come.'

'Great-gran commanded me . . . I think.'

'Have you no mind for yourself?'

I stared up at him. His voice was soft and musical, filling me with fire right up to my ears. 'I would have come anyway,' I admitted, my heart beating madly, 'for I am drawn to you.'

Cat to mouse, my head warned my heart, but Great-gran's latest plan seemed to be growing more clear.

'You are night to my day,' Churen whispered. 'Come, together we shall be the greatest choviars in the world.'

The moon coyly masked her eyes, so there was not much to see with black against black, just a face I could love for ever, and a scarlet belt swirling gently in the evening wind.

Spider to fly, Chime, came the voice in my head. *If you take him you could lose everything.*

'Am I in love?' I asked Churen, longing to reach out and touch him with my hand. 'Are you?'

'Can't you feel the power between us?'

I nodded, but Great-gran's old-time warnings rang clear. *Cat to mouse, spider to fly. Chime, if you take a man as yours, one of you will lose* everything.

Over and over she had told me my heart was not mine to give, over and over, so why was she Cupid-faced now? Between them I felt like I was being super-sucked into a giant pit of tumble-mix.

'Freya, Great-gran has decided, she has chosen me. Take my hand, Chime, feel the power.'

I stepped back. Things were changing too fast. Mary and I agreed long ago never to fall in love. We decided we hated boys. Yet, ever since this incomer appeared, we had both of us grown watchful eyes and scratchy claws, and things were somehow different between us.

'I said take my hand, Chime, feel the power.'

We stood time-link close. He was mine to take, mine to wed, Great-gran had commanded, but if I made a mistake then it would last for ever.

'I have no need to touch you,' I said, knowing that if I once took his hand my heart would butter-melt my skull senseless. 'I feel the energy of your being wherever I go, but is it love?'

Churen offered me his melt-your-heart smile. 'I don't know. Like you, love is new to me, but I long to be sun to your moon, black to your white. Together, we can be one. Think of the gifts we shall share between us then?'

Past to present, plus to minus, came the old-time warning voice in my head. *Only* one *of you will keep the magic. The other will be as nothing.*

'I need time,' I whispered to Churen. 'We both need time.'

'Time I have plenty of,' Churen agreed. 'But, Freya, my spirit has not rested easy since first I saw you and your red-headed friend. While you take your time I will stay very close, be sure of that. When you see Pahn, be sure he hunts for me.'

I said nothing. I knew my heart was called to him. It was like someone had lit a fire in my soul. I was outside child, but inside adult. I knew whatever happened I would love him for ever.

'Well?' Churen asked, moving achingly close.

'Once we are promised, my magic could be lost, or yours. Think of that!'

'We will give or receive. We will know one has made the other. I am ready to choose a wife and Great-gran says the best wife she can think of is you.'

'Now who has no mind of their own?' I retorted. 'Neutral is nothing, for the power of one would suck the other dry and in so doing turn to dust.'

'You want me!'

I nodded. 'But I was called by our people. I am a chime child. I am needed.'

'You are chosen for *me*.'

I couldn't answer him, strange heart-string music filled my ears. He stood so close, his breath sweet as sun-kissed honey.

Marriage, or jumping the broomstick, had never seemed important before, but now my mind flooded with thoughts of Aunt Sally and her posh white house full to the brim with laughing children. I had always thought her stupid, but now at last I understood.

Why should I be different? Why couldn't I taste love?

I couldn't sleep at all that night. The hounds of darkness hunted me, pushing me on and towards something I could not reach no matter how hard I tried. I greeted the first pink strips of morning with relief, and hurried to light our breakfast fire.

'How do you know if you've fallen in love?' I asked Mary as I woke her with hot, sweet tea. I dared not look into her seeking blue eyes.

'Easy!' Mary replied, slurping the sticky stuff with relish. 'You find you've got no brains left.' She watched me carefully as she took another gulp. 'Your brain goes to ashes, your girlfriends don't count for much any more, even special ones, and you never again think JUST FOR YOURSELF.'

'How do you know?'

'Freya, surely *you* know how all those babies came to be in our house! You can't believe that the tooth fairy was promoted, or the gooseberry bushes went into overtime.'

'Of course not!' I retorted, glaring at Mary. 'I've seen loads of baby things born – more than you!'

'Ah, yes,' Mary admitted, 'so you may, but gypsies don't give up everything for a house full of yelling babies. Your mam is practical. She gets on with her life without feeling guilty, and the babies have to help too. Your mam stopped having babies

56

after Pansy, my mum went on almost for ever. My mum acts first and thinks second, and look what happens when you do that! No, being in love is *really stupid,* I think.'

Mary put down her empty cup and stared at me. 'You're not in love are you, Freya?'

'Of course not!' I replied, trying to banish the image of Churen's tapered hand reaching for mine, to ignore the tumble-mix of emotions that had suddenly become me. 'Like you said, being in love is like having a treacle brain.'

8 'Someone's watching us!'

Dibby seemed uneasy the next time we peered through the crystal. She sensed she was being hunted, so she was trying to make sure she chose only the quietest country lanes. If anybody came close she tried to hide Briar behind curtains, hedges or trees. Because of this their journey was slow.

It's not easy hiding a happy-coloured vardo, a neighing horse and a chatting child. The gavver had them spotted with no trouble at all.

'Someone's watching us, Dibbs. I see someone by the hedge.'

'Gavvers!' Dibby said, scowling. 'The police have spotted us.'

58

'Keeping us safe?' asked Briar. 'Looking after us?'

'No,' Dibby admitted, 'can't say they're over fond of keeping gypsies safe. They may be looking for you, Briar, if Mam's panicked and blabbed to Aunt Emma, but most likely they just want to tell us to load up and move on.'

'We'll move on, then?' Briar asked, ever eager to start another day.

'If we can,' Dibby said, scrunching her fingers. 'I hope they don't want to take us back, but I'm frightened Mam's sent them looking for you. I think she's spoiling things 'cause she's scared we can't manage.'

'We can!' Briar said, all big-beam confident.

'Well we could up to now, but a gavver usually brings trouble.'

'Why?'

'Because we travel, we can be blamed for everything. Something stolen? Must be the gypsies. Mess in the hedges? It's got to be the gypsies. Mam says nobody will believe that most of us do our best to be tidy.'

'That's not fair.'

'Who told you life was fair, Briar? Look at me!

It's always, "Be careful Dibby", or, "Let me do this for you Dibby, just this once" (which means for ever!) or, "No Dibby, you better not go with the others, you better stay here".

Dibby's eyes filled with the tears she knew a proper Romany should never shed. 'I was doing really well! The vardo's clean, just like Freya likes it. I'm making sure our tummies are full. I found you a writing stick. We were ever so happy and now things are going badly wrong. The gavver's coming closer. He'll try and take you back. Briar, maybe I'll have no choice but to let you be taken back home.'

'I don't want to go home!'

'Really?' Dibby Gran gave Briar Rose the sort of giant hug that Aunt Emma had practised on me. 'Then, don't worry Briar. I'll think of something, somehow, some way. We *shall* go on.'

The policeman had other ideas. He marched up to Briar, squatted down so he was eye to eye and asked, 'What's your name, little girl?'

'Briar.'

'And how old are you?'

Briar Rose felt Dibby's rib nudge and realised she would have to be very careful indeed. Their travel plans were in great danger. 'Six,' she lied, standing as tall as she could.

'What relation is she?' the policeman asked, pointing at Dibby Gran.

'Mother,' said Briar.

'Aunty,' said Dibby Gran.

The policeman didn't even smile. He just wrote something in his notebook before grabbing Dibby's arm.

'What shall we do!' hot-head Mary shrieked, almost yanking the crystal from my grasp. 'Freya, what shall we *do*?'

I made sure our precious linking crystal was safe. 'Don't pester-panic, Mary, just watch, and then we have a better chance of making a proper plan.'

'I think you had both better come with me,' the policeman told Dibby and Briar firmly. 'Just a few questions, and then I'm sure we'll have this sorted out in no time.'

Dibby took one look at his serious expression and howled in dismay. The policeman's mouth gaped in amazement.

'Madam . . .'

Dibby howled even louder. Suddenly she felt very frightened. She didn't want to be taken away. She wanted Mam and the camp and Briar and me. To Dibby, a gavver was a stranger, no matter how blue his uniform, or kind his ways. Mam had always warned her to have nothing to do with a stranger.

'Look, I'm not going to hurt you,' the policeman said, leading our sobbing Dibby towards his patrol car. 'Now, where is little Briar?'

Dibby stopped crying and looked around. Briar Rose was nowhere to be seen.

'Briar!' Dibby called out desperately. 'Briar, you can't stay out here all alone.'

'I never thought she'd run,' the policeman said defensively. He shuffled uneasily and wrote something else in his little pocket book. 'I thought she'd stay with you.' They stood for ages, and called and called and called, but their voices echoed empty in the trees.

Through the crystal Mary and I saw no sign of our bouncy Briar, just Dibby Gran who was, for the most part, heave-heart hysterical, and the gavver, unable to make her properly calm. It was small wonder that Briar Rose had gone to ground. To her it must have seemed like the end of the world.

'What'll happen now?' Mary asked, all white-face worried.

'Dibby will be taken to the police station and, with any luck, Briar will stay well and truly hidden until we can rescue her.'

'The police will search for her, surely?'

'Of course they will, but they're gorgios, and Briar has learned from us a thing or two.'

'But if they find her?'

I sighed. 'If they find her we search every single foster home until we discover where she's been placed.

'Is it that easy?'

'No, it isn't, but there are lists. Just hope that Briar Rose has the sense to lie still. She could end up being offered to Aunt Emma!'

I wasted my breath trying to make Mary laugh. To her Briar was a silly baby-head with no busy brains at all.

'We should have been closer,' Mary said through scared-to-death chatter teeth. 'If we'd have kept going . . .'

'It's no good feeling guilty about overnight sleeping. If we'd have kept going, there would most likely be two dead horses, and four of us would have been made to answer the gavver's poky-nose questions.'

'I'll kill Dibby when I see her!' Mary told me, almost falling off Elsha in her haste to move on. 'I'll make sure she's never so stupid again.'

'Dibby's not stupid, Mary, she's different.'

'Oh, come on, Freya, Dibby's stupid! All the love in the world can't hide that.'

We rode on in silence for a very long time. Mary was so cross she wouldn't talk, not even when we rested the horses and shared a hunk of bread and some cheese. I felt angry-awkward. Mary is my ages-old friend, and still she hasn't learned that sometimes things just have to happen.

'Where are we going?' Mary asked, when our silence seemed to have lasted for ever.

'Burford.'

'How do you know they are there?'

'I just do. It's a market town by the River Windrush. First we'll find Briar, and then we'll rescue Dibbs.'

'Had we better check through the crystal?'

I shook my head. 'They're safe, both of them. We'll just trot on, there's only five more miles to go.'

Most of those miles were travelled in sulky-face silence. I know Dibby Gran is not piled up with brains, but she'd never willingly let anything bad happen to Briar. It was *because* she loved her so much that she'd needed to travel. We were a pouty-faced pair, Mary and I, and that had never ever happened before. The journey took endless ages.

Dibby Gran was still crying when they arrived at the police station. She was all sob-face red, but *still* they asked her questions.

'Look, you've not been arrested. We'll just sit in the interview room and all you have to do is answer a few small questions, and then we'll find you a nice cup of tea.'

Dibby didn't answer. The policeman edged towards her, Dibby backed away.

'Look, talk to WPC Lloyd. I expect you'll feel more comfortable with a lady officer. I'll just go and organise a hunt for the child. You won't have to worry about her then, will you?'

Dibby sat down where she was shown, folded her hands in her lap, and uneasily prepared to answer questions.

'What's your name?'

'Dibby, ma'am.'

The policewoman looked puzzled. 'What's your surname, Dibby?'

'Gran.'

'You're called Dibby Gran!'

'Yes,' Dibby said proudly, 'I am, and I make the best shoshi sastra pot in the whole wide world.'

'Oh,' was all WPC Lloyd could manage after a while.

'Can I go now?'

'Well, I think you'd better wait, after all, we are trying to find Briar for you.' The policewoman rested her hand kindly on Dibby's. Dibby's hand shot back like a dog-spied rabbit.

'We are looking for a lost little girl called Rose,' WPC Lloyd said, cautiously. 'Are you sure that *your* Briar isn't *our* Rose?'

'There are hundreds of sorts of roses,' Dibby Gran said defensively. 'Mine can't be yours.'

'Your Briar doesn't seem to know if you're her mother or her aunt. You have to admit, Dibby, that is a bit unusual.'

'Well, I think that the name Briar is unusual. I

don't think your Rose and my Briar are the same.'
Dibb's face was fixed, tell-lie blank. I hoped the
gavver just put it down to her having jelly brains.

'Are you sure?'

Dibby burst into tears again. 'I never stole Briar!
I never stole *anything*!' Her whole body trembled with
frustration. 'She's *mine.*'

'You're her aunt. You said so.'

'She's still mine. I'm looking after her,' Dibby
insisted. 'You can't take her. I won't let you.'

'Well, it's not an issue at the moment because
she's disappeared,' WPC Lloyd snapped. 'Now, surely
you're worried about that!'

Poor Dibby looked even more frightened. She
sobbed and sobbed and sobbed.

'OK, Dibby,' WPC Lloyd said, not sure whether
she wanted to pat or slap my frightened gran. 'You
just sit here quietly and I'll go and fetch us a nice cup
of tea.'

'Whatever will we do?' Mary asked as we peered
into the crystal.

'We'll find them. The vardo's happy-coloured and
parked by the River Windrush, we know that. Bryony

will whinny when I call her. Poor Bryony will be starving. It's not often she has to stand still for so long.'

'Forget Bryony, what about Briar Rose?'

'She'll have gone somewhere sensible,' I told Mary to try to stop her shiver-shaking. 'I am a chime child. By the time we reach Burford, I will *know*.'

The crystal had made us talk, but Mary was still knee-knock nervous. We travelled the rest of the way as fast as we could. We both of us knew a small child like Briar had to be found.

Dibby had tried to hide the vardo, but to a Romany it stood proud like a rainbow. Bryony was browsing quietly on the other side of the field. At some point, Briar must have crept back and let her go.

We climbed into the wagon. It was spick-and-span neat, all except for a little pile of neatly snapped twigs.

'Briar was going to light a fire.'

'No,' I grinned, 'close, but better than that. Briar has shown us her patteran. Look, each stick has two tiny slits along one edge. What gorgio would spot that, Mary? Our Briar is a button-bright bunny. Yet again she has left us a trail.'

The patteran sticks led us past the church. Mary didn't even pause.

'You didn't think she'd choose the church then?'

'Too obvious, this sanctuary thing, it's the last place I'd look.'

'We'll make a Romany of you yet, Mary Reed.'

Mary rewarded me with a proper wrinkle-eye smile, the first one for ages. 'I'll tell *you* where she'll be, Freya Boswell. Briar will have gone to the shops. If a policeman appears, she'll attach herself to some busy shopper, who'll never even notice her family has suddenly grown.'

Mary was on-the-ball right. I had no need of chime magic at all. We chose the busiest shop, and Briar just appeared out of nowhere. We laughed in relief and cuddled her close.

'Such a clever girl, Briar.'

Briar Rose smirked. 'I did well, Chime, didn't I? Am I a proper Romany now?'

'As near, I hope, as you're going to get,' Mary muttered, her sense of humour back now Briar was safe.

'She has more to learn,' a voice said from behind the shelves, and out popped Dibby Gran.

Mary and I gaped. Dibby and Briar shrieked in delight. 'We've been waiting for ages! We thought you'd never come!'

'How did you get away?' Mary asked, her head full of images of my blubbering gran.

It was me who felt all parent-proud as Dibby explained. 'They went away. He went to check on the hunt for Briar, she went to find tea. I was crying, they were bothered. They left the door open, so I went.'

'Just like that?'

'Well, a cat helped me.'

'A cat!'

'A black cat with a red collar. It brushed past my legs and stalked out of the door. I thought if the cat could march out, then so could I. I'm far braver than a silly cat.'

'Where did it come from?'

'Gavver's cat. I suppose it lives in the police station.' Dibby looked full-face proud. 'Yes,' she said, 'I walked out just like that.'

'And then what?'

'I followed the cat to the shops. I reckoned it was trying to show me where Briar was.'

'How *sensible*,' Mary said icily. 'If in doubt, follow a cat.'

Dibby shifted her feet uneasily as she glared at Mary. 'Well you're wrong and I'm right! I followed the cat all the way to the toy shop and Briar was there.'

'Wasn't she clever!' Briar said, clapping her hands.

'Yes,' I agreed, 'very clever indeed.'

'Well, if you believe that, you'll believe anything,' Mary told me as we made our way down the hill, mixing in with the shoppers to keep ourselves inconspicuous until we reached the safety of the hedges on the edge of the town. Once there, we melted eagerly into the protective shrubbery to plan our next move.

'They'll be watching the wagon,' Dibby said. 'I'm scared.'

'Take the road towards Lechlade,' I told Mary. 'Dibby should ride Domino as she's the best on a horse. You and Briar ride on Elsha. Go, quickly, and if anyone sees you, chat noisily, as if you have every right in the whole wide world to ride down the lanes. But if a gavver comes, separate. They know Dibby, so will follow her. Domino is fast, the best hedge jumper in the world. You and Briar will have plenty of time to hide.'

'Which way?' Mary asked.

I pointed. 'A mile or so outside town. Stop at our usual place, Dibbs, you'll be safe there. Set up the bender in the copse, then you and Briar can rest, and Dibby can make us all one of her very best shoshi sastra pots.'

'Does it have to be rabbit?'

'Rabbit,' Dibby said proudly, 'is very nice when I make it and, anyway, what else can we find without shopping again?'

Mary raised her eyes to heaven and Briar on to Elsha, all at the same time.

'You'll be all right?' she asked me.

'I'll be back for that stew.'

'Are you *sure*?'

I laughed. 'Mary, don't worry. I'll wait until dark and then I'll have a *wonderful* time. They'll be some wild screaming in the bushes, some violent splashing in the Windrush and, then, somewhere else, I'll light up a field fire . . .'

'No, Freya! That's far too dangerous.'

'I won't just leave it, silly. There'll be a Rom or

72

two hidden around to make sure no real damage is done. By the time the gavvers have sorted all that out, the vardo and I will be long-time gone.

9 'A risk can mean the golden egg'

'You've heard of the crucifixion?' Dibby asked Briar as they sat snuggle-up close to the cooking fire. Briar nodded, so Dibby felt safe to launch into her well-learned legend. 'Well, it was, I am ashamed to say, a gypsy who forged the nails for the cross. Gypsies have always been the best and most reliable metal workers of all. At the time, Jesus was just regarded as a prisoner who was mad enough to think he was the son of God. Anyway, it was a gypsy that made the four bright and shiny nails that were to nail him to the cross.'

'When are we going to tell Dibby and Briar they must go home?' Mary hissed while Dibby was occupied telling her story to Briar.

'Tomorrow . . . Oh come on, Mary, I can't tell her now, not while she's telling Briar a bit of gypsy history. It took her so much practice to get it right!'

'When Jesus was put on the cross they only used three of the nails. One in each hand and one through his crossed feet. Have you been told that, Briar?'

Briar nodded. 'We make crosses at church at Easter, that's when he died.'

I looked at Mary, she was content for the moment. Dibby had grabbed her ears at last and they were flap-back listening.

'Because we made the nails,' Dibby continued, 'we were cursed. The nail that was left over, the fourth piece of iron, stayed burning red hot. There was no escape from it. Wherever gypsies went, the nail followed. It always stayed glowing fiery hot. Smithies poured water on it, the steam blew up and scalded their skin, and it still glowed. It was thrown in streams, making the water hiss and the person who threw it would fall ill, even die. By next morning, the burning nail would appear again, warning, reminding, making us forever move on.'

'What happened?' Briar asked, her face glowing in excitement.

'It just followed. Gypsies of long ago found they had to keep travelling. They were not allowed to settle anywhere, or the burning nail came to frighten them. That nail herded us everywhere, until travelling was locked deep in our blood and we knew no other life.'

'So that's why you're nómadic?' Mary said, forgetting to use her I-don't-believe-you voice.

Dibby nodded. 'Travelling and being made to move on is our punishment for helping to kill the son of God.'

'But you didn't kill him. He rose again.'

'So you say, but that was no thanks to us,' Dibby finished triumphantly. 'Mam says if you do something bad without good reason, you get punished, and that is what has always happened.'

'Taking Briar away without good reason is bad,' Mary said.

'I have to take Briar,' Dibby snapped. 'I have a very good reason.'

'What's so important you have to scare Mam half to death?' Mary asked. 'And what if Aunt Emma finds out? What then?'

Dibby grabbed hold of Briar's hand, as if she

was about to be snatched away from her that very moment. She looked so frightened that I saw Mary's face go guilty glum. 'I have a reason,' Dibby shouted at Mary. 'What I don't have is the words to explain it. Mam will be all right. Great-gran promised.'

'Do you understand that?' Mary asked me crossly. 'Does that make sense to you?'

I had to tongue-tease Mary. She was spout-steam spurting with fury and making me jelly-belly laugh. 'It's obvious,' I said. 'If Dibby doesn't take Briar, she gets chased by the burning nail.'

Mary glared at us all. We all fell into giggle heaps, so Mary stomped off to check the horses.

We made friends quickly enough, for that is our way. 'We have to tell them,' Mary insisted as soon as she thought I might listen.

'Tomorrow. Oh, come on, Mary, Dibbs spent hours making us that lovely stew, then she told Briar stories for ages. I can't tell her now.' Mary was softening. I tried pushing my luck a little further. 'We could just go with her . . .'

'No! We promised your mam we would fetch them back home, and that is exactly what we shall do.'

Mary is a mutton-mule stubborn-head. My great-gran would have to use all the magic in the world to get the better of her. Even though I was cross I had to smother smirk. One day, when Mary was ancient-bone old, she would be the ostrich great-gran of her gorgio world.

'I think we should keep watch,' I said, 'in case the gavvers come back.'

Mary nodded. 'Well, I'll do the first stretch,' she said, struggling to hide a yawn. 'I've had some rest, and you must be shattered, having had to walk back to fetch the vardo.'

I nodded and tucked myself up to sleep. Mary *would* watch. She was still stuffed full of the idea that everything had to be done the gorgio way.

I took over at three. The night was clear and lit by a full-faced moon. I sat outside the bender and watched black-shadow leaves dancing delicately in front of the silver-sky ball, but I was tired and just before dawn I slept.

'WAKE UP!' Mary screeched, pulling my hair in anger. 'WAKE UP YOU STUPID LITTLE GYPSY GIRL. THEY'RE GONE AGAIN!'

I yawned and tried not to let her fury seep into my mind. 'What's the time?'

'Nearly lunch-time,' Mary admitted sheepishly. She should have taken over from me at seven. 'But that's not the point. *You* let them go.'

'How do you know? If you'd have come out earlier . . .'

'If, if, if. It makes no difference. They're gone!'

By now, Mary had burned up all her anger and her scaredness about letting down Mam and Aunt Emma and Uncle Jack. She gave a give-up shrug and sat down beside me. 'So, off we go again,' she said, sounding calmer.

'Yes, off we go again and, like before, Mary, we will find them. There really is no need for you to worry so.'

'Aunt Em and Uncle Jack will be going frantic.'

'No, they won't,' I reminded her as I cleared up our rubbish and made good the ground where we had had our fire. 'They think Kokko George is with us, and I've sent two postcards back already.'

'You can't write like Briar . . . she can only just write.'

'Oh yes I can, so you really needn't wibble-worry at all,' and, just to prove my point, I showed her.

79

'I really can't understand why they crept away in the night,' Mary said, as we packed up our bender, pots and pans, and loaded up the horses.

'Even Dibby is allowed to have reasons. You never know, she might have been chased by the burning nail.'

'I'm not in the mood for your wittering rubbish, Freya!'

'Well, Briar must have been happy to go or she'd have called.'

'That doesn't help us,' Mary said, as I held Elsha's reins and helped her into the saddle. I mounted Domino, who was late-morning frisky, and whispered him calm.

'We'll find some really lovely postcards,' I promised Mary. 'Bilbury is a postcard-pretty place. There's little weavers' cottages by the Painswick stream, and there's a mill.'

'We are not here to look at the view,' Mary reminded me.

'No, but we can sneak a little look, can't we, Mary? Then we'll choose three cards, one for Briar's mum and dad, one for yours and one for Mam, letting her know they are safe, and that last night Dibby made us a really lovely shoshi sastra pot.'

'But we've messed things up and they're gone, Freya.'

'I'm not going to worry Mam by telling her *that*, and if you are deep-heart kind, then you'll shush your mouth too.'

'But that's cheating.'

'No, it's not!' I told Mary firmly. 'It's what Aunt Emma calls a white lie, one designed to make things better. We will take them home safe . . . eventually, exactly as promised.'

Things were all right then. We played happy tourists and chose pretty postcards. Mary insisted on beefburger buns and, while we ate them, we used the crystal to check on Dibby and Briar.

'Lechlade!'

Mary had spotted the town sign and was fearsome furious. 'I bought a map while you were writing your lying little notes. We are nowhere near Lechlade! You're meddling, Freya. You're meddling just like your great-gran. This isn't bad luck, or your Romany magic failing you at last. This is deliberate obstruction, that's what this is.'

I had no glib-lip answer to give. Truth-telling was

well and properly called for now. 'We'll talk over tea.'

We pitched camp. Mary helped me groom the horses, check their hooves and tether them on the side of the lane. 'There had better be a good reason, Freya,' Mary said as we did all this, 'or I shall go straight back and tell Mam and Aunt Emma and Uncle Jack how you deliberately helped them escape.'

Like Dibby, I was sticky-tongue stuffed up for words. I had to find a keep-Mary-happy reason, and it was best that that reason had no mention of my dead, but not sleeping, great-gran.

'Do you remember when you *had* to climb up the outside of Aunt Sally's house to see how your sisters were caring for pouty-faced Penny?'

Mary laughed and helped herself to a huge slice of the chocolate cake we had not been able to resist buying. '*You* wanted to know too. You wanted to know if they had managed to make her better.'

'But I didn't want to scale up the side of the house. I was clucky-chicken scared. You were the one who said it had to be done!'

'We'd been so bored,' Mary mused. 'We needed an adventure.'

'Exactly!' I exclaimed, giving a mind-wink to Great-gran. '*You needed an adventure.* Now, how do you think poor old Dibby feels? She's middle-life years old and yet is treated like a toddle-small child.'

'Well, in some ways she is one.'

'And in some ways she *isn't.*'

'Children have adventures, not grown-ups.'

'Mary, you sound even more ancient-bone old than my great-gran, and she's dead.'

'Your great-gran is the eternal elf. She's capable of having adventures, even when she's dead, provided they cause enough trouble,' Mary teased, 'but that doesn't make it right!'

'Oh please, Mary, let Dibby and Briar have their own adventure. Dibbs might have a mixed-up muddle-mind, but she does have good thinks too.'

'It's too risky.'

'Life is risky. Everyone takes a risk sometimes, especially Mary Reed!'

'Cow!' Mary said with no real malice as we both reached out for the last slice of cake at the same time. I decided to let Mary have it. She was always better natured if her tummy was full.

'A risk can mean the golden egg.'

'Or a million shattered dreams!' Mary retorted, spitting crumbs at me.

'Dibby *needs* an adventure. Are you going to be the one to snatch it away?'

Mary finished chewing her few remaining mouth fragments. I watched with bite-back, baited breath until the very last crumb was gone.

'One thing must happen if they go on.'

'Anything,' I said, crossing my fingers behind my back.

'We follow. We stay very close.'

'Too close and Dibby will know.'

'How?'

'She's a full-blooded Romany, Mary, she'll just know. We could stay one hour away . . . on horseback.

'You promise?'

I promised, and this time I didn't cross my fingers. One hour's ride was a small price to pay, if Dibby could fulfil her I-want-life dream.

10 'I give you the eyes of an owl'

'I think we should make camp now,' I told Mary, noting that her face was a funny shade of pasty-pale.

Mary gave Elsha a firm kick to make sure she took no note of me. 'No! We must go on. I just can't relax until we are close to Briar.'

'*Mary.*'

'Freya, I don't care what you say, we are going on.'

Mary's limbs were shiver-shuddering from gripping her saddle too tight. Her pupils shifted like watery black pools instead of being firm-edged and autumn-sun-sky bright. 'Mary, it's almost dark and anyone can see you are turn-up-toe tired. We have to stop.'

'Ride on,' Mary commanded Elsha, setting her chin as well as Ostrich Gran ever could. 'We'll go on and on and on and on, oh yes we will.'

'We can only travel for one more hour,' I told Mary, giving her a sugar-sweet smile to show I was doing my best to please. 'The horses are wobble-weary too, they need time to rest and graze.'

'We'll see,' Mary said, too worried about Briar and Dibby to care about Domino and the ever-patient Elsha.

'You don't just fill horses with petrol,' I told her crossly. 'Horses need caring for, too.'

Mary said nothing. She just set off after her purposefully pointed chin.

We didn't make the hour! The sandman snatched Mary as we rode. Her eyes snapped sleepy-shut and, before I could grab her, she had crashed to the ground.

'Mary!'

I leaped off Domino and ran to my dearest friend. She lay like a splatter-sprawled starfish, and still she didn't open her eyes.

'Mary!'

I ran my fingers over her body. There was no moan to reward me, but, thankfully, no sign of broken bones. Mary's skin felt fiery hot, even though her colour was flour-dust pale.

I dragged her on to the grassy bank at the side of the lane, and hastily tethered the horses. Elsha carried our water bottle. I snatched it out of the saddlebag and poured some over Mary's face, making sure I wetted her crispy, dry lips, but still she didn't stir.

'Please, Mary,' I whispered. 'Please wake up, Mary, just for me.'

The lane was nowhere-going quiet. I felt shiver-soul scared.

'Wait here,' I told Mary, as if there was a chance she would do something different. 'Wait here.'

Never have I set up a bender so fast. I bent long poles as if they were slither-twigs. I threw heavy tarpaulin over them like it was tissue-paper light. Inside I laid the pillow and blankets that Mary liked to keep her warm.

All this time Mary didn't move a muscle. She lay on the bank as if it was the very best resting-place in the whole wide world. It could have been if the evening sun had just shone warm, and the finger of fever hadn't started to paint her splotchy pink.

Somehow, I managed to drag Mary through the

small gate a bit further up the lane and into the field. I pulled and tugged her like a huge rag-doll, and the very most she did was give one small groan.

Once she was safe in the bender I wetted her lips again and cooled her limbs with the last of our water. Things were very serious now. I needed to fetch water and curing herbs, but I couldn't leave Mary to be snatched by the ghosts of the night.

'I told you I'd never go far.'

I nearly fluster-fainted, I was so startled by the sound.

'Churen!'

He didn't answer. He bent down to study Mary.

'The red blanket shows no signs of breaking her fever, Churen. I need a stronger magic. She should have fresh healing herbs *now*. I dare not wait until morning.'

Churen nodded. 'Only you can make the magic that heals, Chime.'

I nodded, cursing the moon that was not full-face dressed. 'Do you have water?'

Churen nodded. 'Enough for tonight. I will care for her. Now go.'

I turned to leave. The night would not fly easy. It

was not the best time to hunt for burdock, which loves the damp soil of ditches, or to find dandelion, which is best when kissed by the warmth of the sun, or scramble for blackberry, hawthorn and willow to cool the heat of fever.

'I give you the eyes of an owl,' Churen told me, as if it was the most normal gift in the world. 'I give you the swiftness and sure-footedness of the fastest deer, and the nose of a rabbit to smell out the green.'

I felt my eyes grow large and round in the dark. I felt my feet trip with lightness. I heard strange music in my ears and the scent of Churen's body was sweet and strong.

'Great-gran told me you had these gifts but I thought her tongue was tipple-teasing.'

'Go!' Churen said, as if his magic held no importance. 'You will be safe, Pahn will make sure of that, but don't forget that your senses will return to normal with the first shaft of dawn.'

As he spoke he continued to kneel beside Mary, gently stroking her fevered forehead. I felt my heart lurch as I watched those gently caressing hands. I was relieved to see him, glad he was here to help

Mary, but a green-eyed envy cat at the same time.

I left the bender. My brain and my body were all things mixed. The distant trees that banked the river seemed daylight bright. I was soon there with my swift and easy leaping.

The herbs I needed were gathered in no time at all. I had no trouble finding where they grew. Having the sight of an owl meant the night knew no darkness. I just followed my eyes and my busily twitching nose. There was no need of Pahn, and if he did lurk close by, then I did not see him.

'She still sleeps?' I checked as I lit us a fire and put on fresh water to boil for making infusions.

Softly, and creepy-quiet, an owl glided over from the distant trees. It flew so low I had to duck my head as it passed. 'Churen!' I yelled. 'Come quickly! If the owl hoots three times at dawn, Arivell, the god of death, may claim her.'

I shook my head in horror. I could not bear for that to happen. I would give my very soul to protect Mary.

It was Pahn who crept out from the folds of the tent. It was his wide eyes that I glimpsed before he merged back into the protecting darkness. I held my breath, if ever Pahn was needed to prove his hunting skills, then it was now.

The owl was distracted from thoughts of death cries. His eyes followed Pahn, despite the first wispy cracks of flecking pink. Brown eyes to green, green to brown.

Pahn leaped, his long, black body soaring from a lower branch, his teeth bared in warning, his claws unsheathed. The night owl felt his fur as he flapped skywards, landing safely and seemingly unconcerned, just a little further from our tent. Once more, green eyes locked on to brown in a silent battle for Mary's drifting soul.

Once more Pahn leaped. Once more the death owl raised his wings in flight. Even the tree leaves forgot to rustle. It was as if time itself had stopped. Winged bird and outstretched panther hung in the silent sky.

'Moshto!' I called. 'Moshto please help us *now*!'

Pahn fell to the ground spraying out death feathers. The night owl, still silent, flew awkwardly off to find easier prey.

As soon as the crisis was over I took Churen a bowl and we bathed Mary until her skin felt living cool.

By now, my water pot was bubble-boil ready. I poured it over the finger-bruised herbs and prayed that Arivell was gone and Moshto, the god of life, would help me make her well.

> *'Moshto,*
> *take these my herbs,*
> *take this my love.*
> *Wash her fever and sweat in the cool of the*
> *night.*
> *Bring her back to me.'*

When the healing potion was cooled I re-entered the bender. Mary still hadn't stirred. Her skin was now clammy white, her breath feather-fluttered and she lay near-death still.

'Where is Pahn? What if the owl returns?'

'He won't, not until his feathers are grown.'

'Are you sure?'

'Yes,' Churen said, his eyes fixed on Mary. 'It's up to you and Moshto now.'

'Lift her.'

Churen raised Mary as if she was dandelion feather-light. He held up her chin and stroked her neck as I fed her the medicine, just as you would a puppy who needed to swallow but didn't know how.

It took ages to feed her, to make sure she swallowed but never choked. When we had finished I laid some blackberry leaves in a fire-hot tin, so the smoke from their burning should blow close to her nose.

'What do they do?'

'Blackberry is a wonderful thing,' I told Churen, feeling more confident. 'It can stop shiver-shakes and reduce internal lumping. She may have bruised her in bits when she fell, or be swollen inside from the fever.'

'It is time for *you* to rest,' Churen said softly. 'I'll watch while you sleep, then, when it is time for the herbs, I will wake you again.'

We shared the caring time for three whole days. One of us sleeping, one of us awake. Mary either heaved with hotness or lay cold-corpse quiet, but her breathing was even and there was no hoot of an owl to fear-paint the dawn.

I loved to watch Churen sleep. If I closed my eyes I could enter his other world. I could look but not touch, see but not feel. He lay as an innocent child, his body just a shell. At night he was the spirit of woodlands and fields, the guardian of the secrets of stones. Churen was the night hunter, the protector of our night visions. In my dreams Churen and I were already one. Only my daytime mind was fieldmouse shy.

On the third night I could resist the call of my heart no more. I decided to make a token. I would make betrothal ties in blood-tie scarlet. I would make the links that, once he accepted, would bind him for ever. I tore a strip of cloth from his scarlet belt. As he became the fleeting fawn, the flying bat, the hunting fox, I stole from him. Carefully sewing back the tattered edges of cloth, hoping he would not notice his belt was less wide and displayed such a poorly sewn seam.

Herbs have to be gathered fresh to work best, for they heal far better when blessed by the sun, so Churen kept the fire and did most of the day caring, while I went out seeking the things that would make Mary well. In the daylight hours I could not use Churen's magic, so the finding took longer, yet I had the secret satisfaction that there was more power in my own.

Slowly, Mary improved. She began to call out in her sleep. Her long limbs thrashed as her head raced with fever dreams. We would take it in turns to soothe her until, gradually, her body grew just-healthy warm.

On the fourth morning, as I fetched water, I spotted a Romano chirickli washing his feathers clean in the lightly running stream. 'Churen!' I called in excitement. 'I've seen a water wagtail, on the river stones over there.'

Churen raced outside to see. The Romano chirickli was splashing droplets of water everywhere. They glinted like bright jewels on his busily flapping wings. Churen smiled happily. 'You are right, Freya. Now we can be sure that all will be well.'

And it was, for by the time we had gone back inside, Mary was smiling and had shiny, wide-open eyes.

11 'I hope Churen stays for ever'

The days when Mary was recovering were very hard. I looked outside-calm, but inside I was an explosion of confusion. Churen was being so kind, but mostly to her. I wanted her well, really I did, but sometimes, when Churen knelt stroking her copper-dressed head, I could have wished her stone-struck dead!

I felt shut out, doomed to be forever gathering and brewing the things that we needed to make her fully well. Honeysuckle, elder and basil to reduce fever, garlic and golden seal to prevent re-infection and finish the cure. The golden seal had taken me ages to find. I had had to ride over to Cirencester in the end, to a health-food shop. I hadn't thought I'd ever need to visit one of *them* to make someone well!

Soon, Mary was sunshine happy even though her body was weak. All that was needed was time for her to rest. Churen went off hunting deer. We badly needed a change of food, and venison would feed Mary up and help make her sleep-lazy muscles grow strong. The day was summer-sultry warm but we sat by the fire that warmed the water for infusing herbs and would later cook our food. Mary had a blanket wrapped round her shoulders. The family crystal rested in her lap.

'You see, they're quite safe,' I said, wanting to remove the means of Mary knowing what would happen next.

Mary yawned, and continued to watch Dibby pottering around my vardo and Briar staring restlessly at the outside space.

'I think you should rest,' I told Mary gently. 'If you pamper yourself with sleep, your body can make itself well.'

To my relief Mary listened. She handed me back the family crystal and rose.

'I'll bring you some heather tea to soothe you until the sandman comes.'

'When can I have Earl Grey?' Mary asked somewhat testily. 'And normal food.'

I laughed for the first time in ages. Mary was getting more and more lippy-lipped. She was almost better again.

While Mary slept, I lay in the sun sucking freshly plucked grass and mind-travelled back to my vardo. I became the fingers Dibby used to gently dust the shining wood. I became the restless spirit that was Briar. I was the very air they breathed.

'When Freya was small was she allowed to walk where she wanted on her own?'

Dibby thought about lying, I could tell by the way her back stiffened as she cleaned my beautiful, flower-inlaid, wooden surfaces. 'Yes.'

'Did you?' asked Briar, feeling the need for her own bit of space.

'When I was small ... I think.' Automatically Dibby scratched her head where there was a dent forged long ago by unseeing wagon wheels. 'I used to be free ... before the accident.'

'Why not after?'

'Great-gran wouldn't let me. I used to get cross,

not being allowed to run free like the other chavis. Sometimes I went anyway, but someone always made me go back. Then Mam arrived, only she was called Lena then. I named her Lena. Such a pretty name.'

'Mary said that Lena was *your* baby.'

'I'm not sure, I suppose she was. I gave birth to her, but she never really felt like mine. She belonged more to Great-gran.'

'Why?'

'Great-gran was always the one for knowing what was best. Anyway, Mam needed to be minded then. She wasn't fun.'

'Am I fun?'

Dibby smiled happily. 'You are fun, Briar Rose. I always knew that you would be very great fun. Chime said you were the bestest girl of all.'

'Better than Mary?'

'Specially made, she said, so I chose you for my friend. I just want to share a bit of your chavi days.'

'So will you let me go for a walk, alone, like you Romanies do? Can I go out for a while *all by myself*?'

Dibby looked dubious. I was not certain-sure if it was because she was worried about Briar or if she just felt she would be missing out. She wrung her hands, unsure what to do next. 'What, *now*? You want to go now?'

'Please, Dibbs. After all, you used to.'

'Only before I hurt my head,' Dibby repeated. 'Only then.'

'Oh please, Dibby! It's my only chance. Mummy and Daddy will never let me go out alone.'

Dibby giggled. 'No, I can't see Aunt Emma and Uncle Jack letting you run wild in the woods all day.'

'They say it's dangerous.'

'Life is dangerous,' Dibby said, 'but being protected too much is like being trapped like a bird in a cage.' She gave Briar Rose a body-shake hug. 'And that is why you and I are here.'

'It's a big world out here, Dibby.' Briar had stopped sounding brash and was becoming wobble-word worried. 'I'm not sure where to go.'

Dibby Gran laughed. 'What if I gave you enough money for an ice-cream, and told you you could follow the path back through the woods, but I wanted you home long before dark?'

'What will you do while I'm away?'

'I'll make us some supper. Now, take your freedom, Briar, while you can.'

'You won't come after me?' Briar asked, her chin set determined again.

'Of course not,' Dibby promised. 'Sometimes you just have to follow your dreams.'

I was glad the sandman still held Mary gripped in sleep. To her, Briar Rose was a toddle-tongued tot, but even Dibby knew better than that. Briar Rose *is* a truly special little girl. Only her years are baby young.

Romanies are taught from birth to treat freedom with respect, they are wise-ways wary and only really trust their own. They know a gypsy that breaks humanity laws will be savagely sorted by tribe and family. Our Briar is a gorgio-growing girl. She has not yet learned of danger, even though Aunt Emma and Uncle Jack are convinced that behind every bush there lurks an evil stranger!

I have always run free. Great-gran had made sure of that, for a chime child must *be* the wind in the trees, the new life in the fields. Mam had had no choice. If she wanted some peace then I could never be a tethered spirit.

In our family it was Dibby Gran who lost out to tender care. She was a faintly glowing, ever-shielded candle, but sometimes she threw up great sparks of wisdom. She was smiling happily as she let Briar go.

I knew Dibby was right to let Briar taste freedom but the fears of Aunt Emma and Uncle Jack washed strong in my mind. I was taking risks that wrapped all of us.

I closed my eyes and clutched the crystal hug-heart tight. I called in my head the powerful chant that would summon Bastet. To my relief she appeared in the depths of my glass, green eyes glinting. I begged her to watch over Briar, to make sure she felt only joy.

Briar's heart was down-thistle light as she left. She sang her way across the fields and towards the distant village. Once or twice she looked back, checking that Dibby was still by the wagon, and she really was quite free to walk alone.

Dibby didn't watch her go. She busied herself peeling carrots and onions. She set them simmering in a pot with tender rabbit, and added barley, caraway and coriander. Still not satisfied, she hunted about in the vardo, returning with a pinch of dried bay leaf. Dibby dipped and stirred and tasted, and added this and that from her personal bag. The things that made her stews special. The things we had always thought best to let be.

I felt no fear as I mind-shared their world. I knew that Great-gran was not resting quietly in her heaven-happy place because, in her own bossy-boots way, she was trying to unknit life's tangles. But nothing is ever perfect, and I suspected that for every stitch Great-gran was mending, she was dropping another three.

Briar sang loudly all the way to the shops. She sang over the fields, as she clambered over the stile, and all the way down the lane. She smiled so happily at the ice-cream man he filled her cone to overflowing, making her giggle with delight.

As Briar walked to the river bridge she licked round her cone, catching drips. She sat and watched the ripples in the water. She chatted to the ducks and one nosy swan, stopping only to make sure that not a bit of her precious ice-cream was wasted, but she did share the cone or, to be more precise, the swan snatched a bit right out of her hand. The swan was bigger than Briar, so she decided, quite wisely, not to argue.

Only as she left did I sense the intrusion of fear,

for now she had to enter the woods alone.

'Give her courage, Bastet,' I pleaded. 'Give her great joy.'

Briar Rose took a big breath and walked resolutely towards the wood. As she entered the shivering shadows a slinky black cat appeared from the fringing bushes, purring a welcome and brushing her legs to show an eagerness to please. Briar ran her fingers gently down its shining fur. 'You can come with me,' Briar said. 'I'm big, I will keep you safe.'

The sun shone approval. The tree leaves fluttered musically, sending shivers of yellow and green across the woodland floor. Small birds twittered in greeting, a rabbit poked his head up from the ferns and twitched his nose as she passed by. So much was happening that Briar Rose didn't notice that the visible form of Bastet had gone. The magical beauty of the woods had claimed Briar's soul for ever. Her eyes were saucer-wide in excitement as deer and badger, mouse and owl, came in turn to greet her.

She was through the woods in no time at all. Dibby stood ready to welcome her as she skipped across the last field that led to home.

Once Briar had given Dibby a gorgio hug and

started a giggle-pitch chatter about her big adventure, I knew it was time to leave. This was their journey and I was now satisfied that all was well. I returned the crystal, and dropped lavender and lily-of-the-valley oils on Mary's pillow to give the sleep that soothes, but she wakened as I moved.

'Are Dibby and Briar all right? I had the strangest dream. Your mam was catching them in nets . . . like butterflies, and your great-gran kept sneaking up and setting them free.'

'They're fine. The vardo is still where it was, so you can rest easy,' I said. My voice was outside-calm but I was inside bristle-stiff. In my head I was sure Mary was well. Her copper thatch glowed in even the dullest light, and it wasn't fever that was making her blue eyes shine so bright. I was the one that was sick from minding and caring so much. It was my fingers that were green and grubby from bruising herbs, my back that ached from endless seeking and picking, my heart that was sick from the pain of loving both of them so much.

The next morning Mary grimaced as she sipped her herbal tea, even though I had added honey to please her sugar-searching tongue.

'I think perhaps we should follow them now. Dibby is not used to stopping anywhere too long.'

'We'll go soon,' she promised. 'I feel almost well.'

I felt cross. Mary had stopped fretting over Dibby and Briar, her cheeks flushed healthy rose pink, and her whole body shimmer-shone with happiness. I knew she could safely travel, but, somehow, she still managed to convince Churen that she wasn't well. Each time I suggested we move I was made to feel cold-stone heartless, but I dreaded each day I was made to stay. They were growing too close. If he even went to the river to wash, she counted the seconds till he returned.

'We *must* go soon,' I told Mary. 'Dibbs and Briar are ready to move on.'

'You were the one that wanted them to have their own adventure,' Mary said, feigning faintness. 'You were the one that promised they'd be fine.'

I glared at Mary. The thought of love was turning her brain to sticky-up syrup. Somehow I had to set us both free. 'While you have been sick, Mary, things have changed. Dibby is letting Briar run free.'

'Is she safe this moment?'

I couldn't lie. I wanted to, but my tongue wedged

tight in my throat. I gave the smallest nod I could. How could I lie when I knew Bastet followed Briar everywhere, ready to summon the protective powers of Pahn at the merest hint of danger.

'Well you were right then, a bit of freedom is good for her.'

'*You* promised we'd follow, you promised Mam.'

'So I did,' Mary said, 'and we will . . . tomorrow.'

I gave up. Mary was becoming a muddle-brained moron. I could only hope that Churen was really just humouring her to make sure she was well.

I needed space. Churen could escape at night. He could be a rainbow trout in a gently rushing stream, his body soothed by gently flowing fronds. He could be a lone bird caressed by whispering winds in a cushion-cloud sky. But I was bound to Mary by dead Ostrich glue, and even my smile was pasted.

I was an unwilling slave, stood huddled over the steaming kettle cursing granite stones, interfering grandmothers and heart-stealing men.

'I hope Churen stays for ever,' Mary told me while he was busy fishing for supper. 'He's so kind, Freya, he's really special.'

My spine grew pole-metal rigid, my own dreams

of love shiver-shake unstable. 'Do you really like him that much?' I asked, trying to sound light-tone casual.

Mary gave me a funny look. 'Yes,' she said cheerfully. 'I think I do.'

I renewed the hot tin that still smoked blackberry leaves to make sure Mary stayed well. I promised myself never to burn them again for her. 'Are you sure?'

'Yes,' Mary said, looking every bit like a fawning puppy. 'I'm sure.'

'So you mean you're *in love*?'

Mary nodded. 'I think so, but how do you *know*?'

'There are ways to find out,' I told Mary slowly, 'ways we can check.'

'You can find out if he loves me?' Mary asked, her knees huddled up to her chin, her face bright with excitement.

I wanted to shout, He's *mine*, all mine. Great-gran wished it so! but how could I make Mary believe. Great-gran is cold-ash burned and, on top of that, I couldn't really hurt Mary, not when she was only just well.

I stayed all tight-button lipped. Oh, how I have grown. I controlled the dancing fireflies in my belly and said not a single word.

12 'Nine years is for ever!'

Even Mary couldn't pretend for ever. The moment came when Churen told us he must leave. I gave him two red handkerchiefs. I didn't let on that they were made from the silk I stole from his belt. I gave them with love, one from Mary and one from me. He knotted them into his skimpier cummerbund and left us.

Mary rushed into our bender and became a big baby blabbermouth. It was a gorgio thing to do, and even then unseemly. How I wished that Churen had seen her so.

There was no holding us back now. We packed and travelled steadily, quietly, each in a world of dreams.

I suddenly knew we were come cuddle-close to Dibby and Briar. There was no sign of the vardo, no huffing Bryony, or smell of succulent shoshi slowly roasting over a gently smoking fire. My outside eye saw nothing, but my happy heart told me they were only a hair's breadth away.

'Thank God we don't have to go on,' Mary muttered, easing her aching bum from the back of the patient mare. We had travelled well, but she had grown tired.

'Any good at shoshi bashing?' I teased as I helped Mary's trembling legs stand on the firm, sweet earth.

'No! Nor do I want anything to do with hotchi-witchi,' Mary laughed. 'What I want is fish, chips and a beefburger.'

'All at once?'

'All at once. I am so hungry I could eat a horse . . . especially this one.'

'She's too old, and too useful. Are you sure you don't want hedgehog?'

Mary ignored me. She stretched her hands to the sky and yawned.

'You could shuffle down to the village, I suppose, while I put up the bender. Your legs might feel better for walking.'

'Is it far?' Mary asked, looking beyond the line of trees.

I shook my head. 'You'll be back before the fire is lit and the tent erected.'

'Not if I can help it,' Mary muttered, checking for coins before ambling away.

'Don't be too long,' I worry-warned.

'Why should I rush?'

I gave Mary a gentle push. 'Look at the time, silly. You must hurry because a gorgio is always clumsy in the dark. Go on!' I said pushing her harder, 'or those stiff-stuck bones of yours won't reach that far and I shall starve!'

I watched her go, glad to have a quiet space to try to unmuddle my mind. As I set the bender poles into the earth I dreamed of Churen. I felt tenderness closing in tight all around me – me who had always taken such pleasure in running free.

I thought about the cute, cuddly master-magician that we could so easily make, the one that would eventually usurp both Churen and me. Nothing is ever for nothing, I remembered, as I threw the green canvas that would protect us from the elements over the poles. My great-gran had always nag-mouth warned about everything having a price. 'Believe me, Chime Child,' she said, 'you *always* pay.' So what was the cost of love now?

I cut turfs from the ground and laid them carefully under the hedge. I lit us a cooking fire. Churen's eyes burned in my heart as bright as any hungry flame. In my head we stood close again, and he was reaching out for me. If he called again I would not hesitate, I would hold him tight by the welcoming flames. I would love him for ever. It was not the smell of burning wood that filled my nostrils, it was the odour of full fleshed man.

My heart hurt so much that I was almost relieved when Mary returned with her basket of gorgio goodies, and I was happy not to have to bother to cook properly too. Sometimes, it's nice to have things out of packets and bags, and do no work at all.

'If one of us ever did marry Churen,' Mary said wistfully as she paused from stuffing her face with fire-roasted beefburger, 'would your magic tell us when?'

'When is easier than who,' I said, stomping out the last remains of our fire, 'and you've asked just in time.'

'It's gone eleven!'

'Well,' I said, goofy-grinning at the thought of a small diversion, 'we have to be there by midnight.'

'Where?' Mary peered curiously into the cloudy night.

'Across the fields, through the woods and towards Orchard Farm.'

'How far?'

'Three miles by road, one as the crow flies.'

'You're joking!' Mary was two-way torn. One bit of her longed for her nice warm bed, the other was desperate to know the secrets of her wedding day.

'We'll have to hurry. It's dark, not easy to travel, but if you'd rather sleep . . .'

Mary closed up our bender. 'Some things,' she said, 'you just have to find out.'

We ran across the fields. We raced each other over the gate and ended up in a fat-giggle heap on the other side.

'This field is fed by the river,' I warned Mary. 'Take care. Even in summer it hugs water.'

The clouds hugged the moon close so it was not easy to see. I could tell where the boggy bits were in time, for my tread was light, my naked toes sensitive to the touch of cold. Mary's shoes protected her feet, but left her unable to feel. She soon stumbled, ending up muddied right up to her knees.

'Still want to go on?'

'Of course,' Mary declared, rubbing her grubby knees with her hand and then obeying an irresistible urge to scratch her nose. I didn't need the sun to know that even Churen would giggle if he could see her now.

The river was wide but shallow, and straddled by shiny, wet stepping-stones. 'Will you steady me?' Mary asked, still slightly shaken from her tumble, for the stones looked sheeny and eerie, edged up with lightly bubbling water. Our eyes were night-time adjusted, but still we had to struggle to see. We made it halfway, but by then it was more like skating than walking and we were hooting with laughter, so much so that we failed to take care.

'Oh, sugar!' I screeched, feeling my balance topple-tumble away. Mary was guffawing so much she forgot to let go of my hand, so we ended up in a tangled muddle-mess in the heart of the cold, frothy stream.

'Do you want to go back?' I asked. 'There is no time to leaf-scrub dry.'

'Nope!' Mary set her chin. 'Since when have we ever given in to a spot of trouble?'

Mary was right. We were no faint-heart fairies. We pulled ourselves up, shook like dogs, and waded the rest of the way across, then scrambled up the gently sloping bank on the other side. We were so cold we fair galloped across the field on the other side and in no time at all we had entered the wood.

'Which way?'

'North.'

'How can you tell?'

'The stars.'

'There aren't any.'

'Well it was worth a try,' I admitted. 'Take it from me, I just know.'

'So, you've been here before . . . nothing to do with stealing the odd egg, Freya, or even the odd hen?'

I grinned and gave Mary a shove. 'Now really, Mary, as if I would do that!'

Night woods can be very scary-dressed. Even the rustling leaves in the trees sound like a million flustered ghosts determined not to let you by. I wondered if Pahn paced protectively in the shadows

115

beside us. I saw no sign of him. We were very cold from getting so wet. There was certainly no Bastet to bring us joy.

'I'm frightened,' Mary admitted when we were three parts there.

'We'll make it if we go on. We can take our time coming back, take the lane that winds back to our road.

'I can't go on.'

'Yes you can! When did *you* ever give in to a dare?'

An owl hooted, a cat wailed, a rat ran towards the river. The spectres of the night were serving it well. Mary stopped in her tracks, her feet fear-switched to stone.

'Come on! If I let you stop now you'd curse me for ever.'

'We could go another night, when there is more time and the moon is full.'

'You can only try each magic once and, for you, the magic has started now! It started the moment you set your heart to come.'

Mary took a deep breath, her face shone grey in the blackness.

'Mary Reed, I dare you!'

Mary held my gaze but didn't move. One bit of me would have been quite happy to see her stop, but she was my friend, and we had agreed years ago to be friends for ever. I could not let her lose face on such a simple challenge.

'Mary Reed, you are a great clucky chicken! Cluck cluck cluck! I shall leave you alone.' I pretended to go. Mary had no choice. Her panic thoughts of being alone were greater than her terror of moving. Stone became feather and we raced our way out of the woods on the wings of Mary's fear. The night seemed almost bright when we emerged the other side.

'What now?' Mary asked as our bodies steamed from the strange mix of hot-blood insides and water-cold skin.

'Only one of us can do this magic. The next bit is not far, but you have to go alone.'

Mary shivered. 'Is it worth it? Will I really know?'

I nodded. 'Look, the rest is almost easy. You have to creep over to that shed over there. Inside, the hens are head-tucked roosting. Now, listen carefully. You have to be as quiet as a church mouse until you get there. Once you have arrived, you have to stay lock-lip quiet until your watch shows exactly midnight.

'Then?' Mary asked, all outside suspicious and inside jelly-legged.

'Simple. You stand up. If the hens cackle then you won't marry, but if the cock crows, then you will.'

'But I want to know *when*.'

'When is easy. You stand perfectly still until the cock stops crowing. Every time the cock doodles you have to wait one year. Only when you are sure he has stopped are you free to go.'

Mary checked her watch. She had seven whole minutes. Alone in the dark seven minutes is a very long time.

I still dared not leaf myself dry or wring out my clothes, in case I woke the sleeping hens. I sat myself down at the edge of the field and tried to shut out the shiver-trembles that kept wanting to grip me.

I watched Mary edge on her belly to the side of the roost. There was now only one minute left to go. In those last sixty seconds it felt like the world had stopped. Even the whisper leaves forgot to breathe. Every bit of air was still.

Mary rose to her feet, and in the silence of the night her movement was thud-foot loud.

For a moment, nothing happened. No clucking hen, no hint of a cackle or crow. Mary frowned and turned her head.

Cock-a-doodle-do!

She would be smug-face pleased now, secure in the knowledge she would some day marry.

Cock-a-doodle-do!

Cock-a-doodle-do!

Mary and I counted carefully. The bossy boy bird was harem-hen furious that someone should dare to creep up in the night and stand so close to his feather-dressed girls.

'Nine years!' Mary called as she raced back across the fields. 'Nine years is for ever!'

'At least he crowed,' I reminded her. 'At least you know you *will* wed.'

'Nine years!' Mary kept muttering as we found our way to the lane that would lead us home. I was glad that the dark hid my smile.

If Mary had to stay single for nine whole years, then there was still a good chance that Churen was meant for me.

13 Churen come, Churen stay

'Have you any money?' Dibby asked Briar, frowning as she shook her head. 'Not even a penny?'

Briar dug even deeper into her pockets. 'No.'

'Oh, well!' Dibby said. 'Our next adventure has to be to turn you into a proper gypsy.'

'I *won't* beg!' Briar set her chin firm, looking every bit as stubborn as Mary as she glared at Dibby.

'We don't beg,' Dibby said, rooting around in the cupboard to the left of the small, shiny, black and almost never-used stove. 'We sell.'

'I can't see any lucky heather,' Briar said, poking her button nose into the cupboards on the other side.

I felt panicky-possessive. My tummy trembled

with crossness. I loved them both dearly, but the vardo was *mine*. I tried to shut out the little voice in my head that said, *Take them back to Mam, just like she said, and then once again the vardo will be yours, all yours.*

'No, there's no heather, so we shall have to do something different. We shall have to dukker.'

'What's that?' Briar asked, her little head bobbing at the thought of an adventure.

'Tell fortunes.'

'I can't tell fortunes.'

'I can,' Dibby said proudly. 'Not like Freya, of course. She will never sell her skills because they're mostly healing, unless she senses a self-pitying fool, and then she'll make them pay highly for her skills. She says that sort only believe something will work if it costs them dear.

'I'm not like Freya, but I can dukker. I can guess really well what people want to hear for a pound or two. I am able to tell fortunes because Urania Boswell was an ancient of ours, and it was her who grew famous from knowing when Queen Victoria was going to die.'

'Who's Queen Victoria?'

'I don't know, an old queen who wore black, I think. Urania Boswell was very clever. She predicted that people would fly in the air and travel under water long before they actually did.'

Briar gave up inspecting cupboards. 'Did she guess?'

'No, how could she have guessed that a big liner called the *Titanic* was going to sink? She warned several people who came to her not to go on the ship. "You will die," she said, and because she had been right so many times before, they listened ... and lived.'

'Do you know when bad things will happen?'

'No, but Mam says, if I hadn't banged my head ...'

Dibby wrapped my most brilliant headscarf round her neck, making my tummy scrumple-twinge once more. She borrowed my best golden sovereign earrings and stuffed them into the holes in her ears. Finally, she sagged her shoulders to hunch them round. Such simple things changed her from looking ordinary to looking mysterious. The gorgios would sense strangeness and prefer to offer a coin than walk away.

Dibby offered Briar a large, shiny, patterned pebble, the sort you can find with care on any beach.

Briar reached out to take the pebble, but Dibby held it just out of reach.

'I see luck coming to you, lady, so cover my palm with silver to fetch in your good fortune, or better still, lady, give me some of that paper money that serves you so well, and then I can tell you more.'

'We haven't got any money!'

'For goodness sake, Briar! *Pretend.*'

Briar Rose tore up two strips of food-wrap paper and placed them in Dibby's hand. She reached out to take the travelling stone, but Dibby still wouldn't let it go.

'Less haste, lady,' Dibby said. 'Let your hand rest on mine. You'll come to no harm.' She studied Briar's hand carefully. 'Lady, I see you have had many troubles lately. The world has been very hard for you, something has made you sad.'

'How do you know I've been sad?' asked Briar.

'You're not pretending very well!' Dibby said crossly. 'If you were a middle-aged lady, the sort that pays best, the odds are your hands would look worn, your nails bitten or your face furrowed. Something about you would give me a clue and, anyway, almost everyone has been sad about something.'

'My family *have* caused me lots of problems,' Briar admitted. 'Mummy and Daddy have moved house and I do miss them. I'm in the care of a really dibby aunt. I'm having fun. She's ever so funny. If she wasn't . . . I'd go home.'

'Your problems will be over very soon,' Dibby said, not batting an eyelid. 'Yes, lady, something wonderful is about to happen, something you were really hoping for. I see your parents returning, and you will have a brother and sister to play with, so things will sort themselves out very soon.'

Briar tried to withdraw her hand, but Dibby held her just firmly enough for her not to feel free to remove it. 'Now that's a pretty ring you are wearing, lady. Give me that ring for luck, and then I can promise you a really big slice of fortune.'

'It belonged to my mummy,' Briar pretended, 'so I just couldn't give it away.'

'No matter,' Dibby said lightly, 'some more paper money will serve just as well.'

Briar reluctantly handed over another two notes. 'That's all that I have,' she said, 'honestly.'

Dibby pocketed the paper money without seeming to notice its value, and without letting go of the

124

travelling stone or Briar's hand. 'As I said, lady, luck is about to change for you.' She gripped Briar's hand more tightly and stared intently into her eyes. 'Now, my dear, to change your fortune you must make three wishes. You must make them holding my hand, and you must never speak them aloud. By the time the next Christmas has passed, they will all have come true.'

Briar and Dibby held both eyes and hands for a moment before Dibby broke contact and gave Briar the stone. 'Take this, lady, and keep it always with you, for where you and the stone travel, luck will be with you.'

Briar took the stone and put it into her pocket. Dibby grinned at her. 'Did you make three wishes?'

Briar giggled sheepishly, then nodded.

'See, I told you! *Every gorgio believes.*'

Briar chuckled, sounding more confident now. 'They might be pretending to believe . . . in case you curse them.'

'It doesn't matter,' Dibby said. 'Either way, the money is ours.'

I longed to stay and see what happened but Mary was calling me back to her here-and-now world. 'Do you think I should fetch the crystal to check on Dibby and Briar?'

'Oh, you remember the reason we travel then?'

Mary looked guilty. It was a long time since she had worried about Dibby and Briar. 'I'd better fetch it.'

'No need!' I said, putting down the brush I had used to groom the horses while lost in my mind-travel time. 'They are safe and well.'

I didn't want her to look into the crystal. I was sure it was best that she shouldn't see Briar dressed up in a slightly tattered frock with a carefully placed streak of mud on her face. Briar didn't *need* to beg. She *looked* really hungry. As each gorgio passed she gave them a sad, hopeful look. In no time at all, Dibby and Briar had gathered a crowd.

'I wonder what they're doing for money,' Mary said, stroking Elsha's muzzle. 'They must have run out by now.'

I stared at her all open-mouth gaped. She was learning the Romany ways; she was learning to dip into the waves of thought that continually wash the mind.

'You've seen me sell posies of flowers,' I said.

126

'Or herbs for cooking, or fancy coloured medicines to make those that wallow in sickness feel well.'

'Dibby and Briar seem unlikely salesmen.'

'You're wrong!' I told her as we mounted up ready to go. 'They're doing really well.'

Now that Mary was lippy-lively again, we made very good time. I paced the horses fast, but made the days short, that way Mary was not over-much tired and the horses kept fit and well.

We were happy between us again, for there were long days when Churen was nowhere to be seen.

'Can you tell if I'll marry *him*?' Mary asked when we stopped to enjoy cheesy baked potatoes for early supper. 'If it's him I'd wait for ever!'

'There's an old-time way,' I said, my mood good from munching contentedly, 'but it's you that will have to go gathering sticky old clay.'

Mary would do anything for love. Her brain had jellied to nothing. She trotted off as if it was the most normal thing in the world for an almost-grown girl to go gathering clumps of messy old mud.

I lay on my back by the no longer needed fire, closed my eyes and chewed on a piece of freshly plucked grass. Bees hummed over sweet evening clover, but to me it was Churen's strange music that was filling my ears.

I was back at Rollright Stones, reliving the moment when our fingers almost joined, feeling the power that would surge through me the moment I dared to take his hand. Strong, dancing lights magic-flickered eagerly over the granites, waiting to be released by our joining. Powerful forces were waiting to enfold us with pleasure, delight us, consume us. 'He's *yours*!' Great-gran was saying, her voice as solid as those blocks of time-worn stone. 'Yours to take, yours to use one day to make a chime child of your own.'

'Found the clay!' Mary said, breaking my dream. 'Now what?'

'You have to write our names on strips of paper and carefully wrap each one in a ball of clay.'

'Both our names?' Mary checked, giving me that meaningful look again.

'Both our names,' I said firmly. 'For how can it work with just one?'

Mary did as she was bid, clamping the clay firmly round each name, so it was lost from sight. I watched carefully, making sure she didn't play up and put extra clay round mine.

'Hold tight to the ball that is named Churen,' I told her. 'Drop our balls into a shallow bowl of water, have the balls just covered . . . like so. Now repeat all the time the clay is melting:

> *'Churen come, Churen stay,*
> *She who floats will rule the day.*

'Say it over and over until you can read the first name that clears from the clay.'

Mary started chanting. I didn't want to look, but was drawn all tumble-mix trembly to the tagged balls of clay.

'It's mine!' Mary yelled excitedly. 'It's going to be mine!'

'No! It's *mine*,' I said, my eyes bright with hope. 'The paper that has uncurled most is mine.'

Mary forgot to chant. She grabbed my shoulders and shudder-shook me. 'We're supposed to be friends and you never *said* you loved him too!' She was yelling and swaying and red-faced with rage. 'Don't try and deny it, gypsy girl. I can see by your face you *do*!'

I tried to shake my head, but we both knew I lied.

Mary's temper had flared and died but she was still scowling. Eventually, she turned back to look at the melted balls of clay.

Our names lay open together, Mary and Freya, Freya and Mary. She looked full-face furious, but I was secretly pleased. There was still some hope left . . . for both of us.

14 'I shattered the glass'

We met up again at Marlborough. Dibby greeted us with delight, once we had promised that her journey could continue, and we would not stay with her every single step of the way.

For one precious night the vardo was mine. Briar wanted to sleep in the bender, so Mary and Dibby had chosen it too, so determined were they to stay close to their rambling Rose.

The moon was full-face happy again, and I was pleased. There was time for me to make a little magic of my own.

I closed the wagon doors and drew the curtains, shutting myself into my own private world. By the light of a candle I spread a black cloth over the cupboard that also served as a table. The black silk had no witchcraft-evil intentions, it was just to make sure that tricks of the light did not muddle my questing brain.

Once I was satisfied that there were no reflections to interfere with the reading ways, I filled a tumbler right up to the very brim with fresh, sweet water. I placed it in the centre of my table, being careful not to spill a single drop.

To the left of the glass I put a newly lit candle, to the right a jasmine taper. Now at last I was ready. I blew out the preparation candle, closed my eyes and repeated the ancient Romany words three times.

Scry scry scry for me
Bring the face that I must see.
Let me gaze on my future mate,
To know which lover will be my fate.

I gazed all anxious impatient into the flames, but strike-heart pain was my reward for delving in magic ways. There was no image of Churen leaning idly against the ancient granites, his lips scrunched up and ready to tease. There was no sign of any amorous Rom at all!

The augur glass was filled with gypsies and gorgios, all clustered round my vardo, all calling me. The only loving hand clutching mine belonged to little Briar.

It can't be! I told myself. Great-gran does not wish it so.

I willed the images to change, for Churen to march through the endless stream of Romanies and claim my hand. The only thing that happened was that the apparition of Briar Rose smiled and asked me to teach her my magic.

'This can't be my destiny,' I told the flickering candle. 'To be in a crowd and yet always alone.'

You are a chime child, came a voice in my head. *You are needed by your people.*

'But I want Churen! With Churen I can be happy. Together we can make the greatest choviar in the whole wide world.'

We have no need of Churen, the voice of the people screamed. *You have magic enough for us all. The chime child of the future will come forth when needed. It will rise from the line of Briar Rose.*

I shattered the glass, and with it a million dreams. I stalked out into the night that was too warm to cool the tears I could not even shed. For endless hours I walked the woods alone.

Churen was everywhere: in the trees that whispered comforts in the whisper wind; in the dew that wetted my toes and reminded me of the sweetness of the earth; in the rustling of a rabbit and the scent of a watchful deer.

My people still needed me. I could not escape my calling. I was tied up tight with love and expectation. I am a choviar, and up until now, that is all I ever wanted to be.

I had always felt like a free spirit, at one with the mysteries that only Churen could really share, night to day, past to present, thoughts found and lost. Now I realised that I too was bound by family threads. I was tied up so tight I could never simply be me.

I am chosen. I have no choice but to hold my head up proudly, but my inside seams crack with the quiet seeping of salty tears.

15 Stonehenge

'Are all Romanies mad about stones or just your lot?' Mary asked as we spied on Dibby and Briar from the side of the road that bordered Stonehenge.

'Just our lot, I expect,' I admitted.

'Good, because I think stone worship is dead boring.'

'We don't stone worship!' I told Mary crossly. 'We stone appreciate. These stones were fetched from Ireland by Merlin, and he was the greatest magician of them all.'

'You might consider yourself the best choviar in your Romany world,' Mary told me sourly, 'but I think all witches, black or white, meddlers or magic makers, should be burned at the stake.'

'Why?'

'Freya, I was born to ride on buses. I've got blisters on my hands, I've got bruises on my bottom. On top of that, I've almost drowned in herbal tea and my lungs are full of burning leaves, and you, the greatest choviar in the whole wide world, ask me *why*!'

'You didn't have to come,' I said, pulling Mary behind some Americans as Dibby glanced our way.

'Well, there was one good thing about coming,' Mary admitted.

'What?'

'Churen Isaacs! That silly red belt of his seems to tie him to stones . . . so I'll come.'

'You really do fancy him,' I said, trying to tingle tease, 'so much so, you have scrambled your brain to chutney.'

'Yes,' said Mary, with not a hint of humour, 'I really do fancy him. The only problem I have, is so do *you*.'

We stood close-friend near, but felt driven apart. It was a time for silence, a cooling time.

'This is Stonehenge,' Dibby told Briar, as she waved her hand at the huge circle of granite. 'Now what do you see?'

'A pile of crooked old stones,' Briar replied, sounding every bit like Mary.

Dibby led Briar closer. 'Now what do you see?'

'Even bigger stones, and lots of wire to stop you reaching them.'

Dibby nodded sadly. 'When I was small you could walk under these stones. You could really *feel* their power.'

'They looked lots nicer when they were further away,' Briar Rose said, watching all the people milling about. 'When we saw them sitting all alone in the middle of the fields, they looked bigger, as if they owned everything. I'd feel lonely all by myself. Can stones feel lonely, Dibby? Do they like us to visit?'

'Salisbury Plain is their space. A ring of barbed-wire is wrong and the stones are sad. They belong to the people. Can't you feel anything?'

'Too many people, all too busy,' Briar said, grabbing Dibby's hand.

'I don't like these stones any more,' Dibby confessed. 'They are not living properly now. You can't touch them and ask for help when you need to. It's only in the distance you see how they should be.

Standing by the wire they look like cold, grey captives. I *wish* you could stand underneath them, Briar. When you are that close they are truly magnificent again. If you could just hug the granites, especially the blues, you would know how their magic is sucked dry by the wire.'

'Magic?' Briar asked, watching a sea of tourists stomp round the edging boundary. 'What magic?'

'People used to see strange lights, quite often. I have done myself. Sometimes your ears fill with music, or there are strange clicking noises. Well, there used to be, when they were free to give and take in the snakes and ladders of life. In the old days, anything could happen. The stones would talk to you, if you reached out to them with your heart. They had living ways.'

'Too many people for that,' Briar said, and I felt proper proud of her Romany-thought ways. Our Dibby was teaching her well.

'Now they are just a monument, but the streams of life still run hidden under Stonehenge,' Dibby said, more to herself than Briar. 'Nothing happens here now, though. Everything is sleeping.'

'So why did you bring me?'

'Because I wanted you to *see.*' Dibby scratched the hidden dent in her head. 'No, I wanted you to *feel.*'

'I don't feel anything,' Briar said sadly.

'Exactly!' Dibby exclaimed triumphantly. 'Now you feel nothing. They put up the wire to save the stones from the people, but the stones *need* the people, just as the people need the stones.'

Briar Rose looked once more at the henge, and then turned back to Dibby. 'So it is better to be useful and one day die than to take no risks and live for ever . . . even for stones.'

'Exactly right, Briar, even for stones.'

16 Acorn cup and ashen key

Churen Isaacs had not appeared for ages and Mary and I both pined for him. Sometimes it was hard to stay friends, both of us wanting his company so much, but sometimes it made life easier. We could share our heart ache. It was in one of our sharing moods that I told Mary how I could fetch him back.

'It's an ancient way.'

'Anything!'

'It will only work if one day he will choose one of us to jump the broomstick.'

'Do you really jump broomsticks?'

I laughed. 'Not usually, that's gorgio legend mostly. My people just go off with their chosen partner for the whole night. Only the man we will wed mind, there must be no mistake. When we return we are considered married. We confess we eloped, get forgiven, and are, from then on, joined for ever.

'No divorce?'

'Divorce is very rare, a total loss of honour. You have to choose your partner well, be sure you can make the marriage work.'

'Why do you have to elope then?'

'To a Romany, marriage is the joining of *families*. Once, almost all marriages were arranged. In those days, the great-grans of this world would choose who would jump the broomstick with you before you were even born. Even now, Mam will have one idea who I should wed, Tashar will have another, Vashti a third. All of the family will think they know best. This partner will bring wealth, that one great skill, the other the very best luck.'

'Sounds very political. I shall choose my own man.'

'So will I, when I am ready. Every Romany chavi chooses her man, that's *why* we elope. When we come back there is dishonour if we are not accepted by our families, so the politics are forgotten and everyone is happy.'

'So *who* gets Churen, you or me?'

'We will only know when the time is right,' I said, blocking the glass magic from my mind, 'but we can call him back if it is to be. We each need a piece of oak with an acorn attached, and some ash that is shaped like a key.'

'That won't be easy!'

'It's not impossible,' I said, needing Churen every bit as much as Mary. 'The acorns don't have to be ripe, and they could be from last year. The ashen key is best with hanging seeds, but we could carve the shape from living wood. It would be very much easier to work this magic in autumn.'

'I can't possibly wait until autumn. I shall be back at school in September.'

The road to Avebury took us along country lanes, but an oak with acorns was very hard to find. Dibby and Briar were growing more than an hour away, but Mary didn't seem to mind. She was at one with me in the need to make magic. Eventually our patience rewarded us, and I started the charm.

We each placed a piece of oak, with its acorn, and an ashen key under our pillow. Before we slept I lit a candle. We placed it between us, and gazed into the flames chanting the calling words I had taught her . . . together:

> *Acorn cup and ashen key*
> *Bid my true love come to me.*
> *Over meadows, over moor*
> *Bring back the man that I adore.*

For three nights we repeated the calling words, staring intently all the while into our candle flame.

While I gazed into the gently flaring, yellow light I tried to shut out the images of Great-gran that danced in the flame. I could see her in her watch-the-world chair, delighting in the turmoil she was causing with her meddlesome ways.

'When will he come?' Mary asked, her face flushed with excitement.

'Between moonlight and firelight,' I said, damping the impulse to smash up her head.

We waited and waited. My outside face wore calm, but deep down my mind had melted to mud, like Mary's.

The finger of time passed bored-snail slowly. The moon rose and the night grew cool, but still we dared not light ourselves a cooking fire. We willed him to come on wings of hope.

He came on a cloud of red ribbon.

'I am summoned?'

Mary giggled. 'We needed you, Churen. We *missed* you. How could you leave us when we have learned to like you so well?'

I glared at Mary. It was not seemly to lay open so soon the secrets best left in the depths of your heart. It had been different for me. Great-gran had commanded. Great-gran had *wanted* me to take his hand.

'I needed to be one with the night,' Churen said. 'Sometimes I feel like I am being torn in two.'

'Not by us, I hope?' Mary teased, her face flushed with happiness at having him so close.

Churen said nothing. I felt the emptiness of fear. We were red-web entangled. One of us bound, one day, to gain our heart's desire, the other doomed to soak a pillow with lonely tears.

'Are you hungry?' I asked, needing the security of routine. Churen nodded. I retreated into the night to kindle the fire. Twice I had had the chance to make him mine, and twice I had let him go.

'Have *you* ever been in love?' I heard Mary ask him, her voice failing to hide the edge of desire. Oh, how I wished I was Mary-mouth confident, but I was a tumble-mix of love and fear, and knew exactly why.

I, who had always taken what I needed from Mother Earth, had discovered love was mixed with frizzle-fright fear. An offered heart is not a gift accepted lightly. It is a burden to cherish for ever.

'Love is not simple for me,' Churen said as he led Mary outside to sit by my fire.

'Love is very simple,' Mary told him. 'You just give.'

'You're wrong. Love is always complicated,' Churen said softly, as he gazed into the flickering flames. 'There are always strings. Once I wrap myself in a security blanket of love, I lose everything that has ever been me.'

I kept my face still as I fiddled with our kettle hook. He was afraid too, his heart thinks sounded more than a bit like mine.

'You'd lose total independence,' Mary agreed, 'but you'd gain more. My mum says having kids produces all the problems in the world, and I used to think her mad to have so many, but she always added that, at the end of the day, children are the future, they are all that really matters. Now I understand her.'

'I would like children,' Churen admitted, 'but imagine not being able to soar in the heavens like a bird, or hunt in the night like a tiger, or see like an owl.'

'I can do none of those things, and neither can you, except in your dreams,' Mary said firmly. 'There comes a time when you have to live in the real world and do your best to be happy.'

Churen patted her shoulder but stared at me. His eyes dragged me closer, inviting me to join in. I blocked up the holes in my heart and offered him tea.

Churen sat back on his haunches and mused as he drank. 'If I were to fall in love with you, Mary, I would have to give up everything exciting, but I could find myself content for ever.'

He tossed some dry grass into the flames and watched them flare up brightly, curl and die. 'If I choose you, Freya, our love would be as the leaves, intense, instant and gone. Our magic would frizzle to dust, for I am the night and you are the day. When one holds the power and the other is nothing, love can last only a moment. Apart, one of us can hold the ancient secrets of the earth. Together we are doomed to burn out, be consumed.'

'Be content with me?' Mary pleaded, not even bothering to hide her delight that the odds against Churen and me were stacked so high. 'Content can be wonderfully happy.'

'If I choose Freya,' Churen continued as if she hadn't spoken, 'and before the flames of love died we made a child, then our baby would be the most powerful choviar of all. Imagine that!'

I did not *have* to imagine. Great-gran appeared in the flames, triumphantly holding a gift-wrapped baby. *Her* future secure in *her* arms . . . but I wasn't there, and neither was Churen. We were the scattered black embers that fell to dust round her celebration fire.

'Whatever I do,' Churen said sadly, 'I will not remain me. Not unless I stay alone for ever. I cannot be fully mortal *and* share the magical enchantment that is given by Pahn.'

I knew that Mary would never understand. She saw him as solid and dependable. To her, he would be the father of her future. The sharer of her dreams. She *knew* she could make him happy.

I saw him shimmering and sensual as mottled

moonlight, and just as soon gone. I knew that common sense said let things be, but still I yearned for him.

'It's not yet time to choose,' I said, hoping that time would make me wiser. 'The time for marriage is far away.'

'It's never too soon to make plans,' Mary replied. 'Plans never hurt anybody. If you let just one chance slip through your fingers, it is gone for ever.'

17 Avebury

'You are right,' Briar told Dibby, as Mary and I watched them through the linking crystal. They were skipping hand in hand round the deserted stones in the moonlit dark, just them, a few sheep and the stones.

'Avebury is really exciting at night.'

'Why?' Dibby asked, settling herself down against one of the larger columns so she could catch her breath.

'Well, if you stop skipping and stand close to them in the quiet, they talk.'

'I told you they were miles better than Stonehenge, even though they are much smaller. These stones live among the people, loved and protected but *free.*'

Briar Rose settled herself down next to Dibby Gran, who instinctively wrapped her arms tight round Briar in the gorgio way.

'I listened and the stones told me lots of things, Dibby. I got told about girls and boys who touched each one to try and keep together. I hate boys so that's got to be silly hasn't it? I heard children giggling as they played hide and seek. It was like looking into an egg-timer: kids in strange clothes, in sands of time. Can we join in and play hide and seek too?'

'We certainly can,' Dibby chuckled. 'There are lots of places to hide.'

'The stones told me that the sheep have been here for thousands of years, just like they are now. I like sheep. Nothing has changed much, they said, and they whispered of barrows close by. What are barrows, Dibby?'

'Abandoned homes for old-time dead, I think,' Dibby Gran told Briar after some thought. 'I've only seen them empty. Their ghosts sometimes linger, but their bodies have long since gone. I think the best one is at Wayland's Smithy. Yes, I shall take you there. We can leave the ghost a shilling.'

'Will we see Silbury Hill? The stones told me all about that. They were really proud because it was built by hand, and sometimes the workmen came to tell them all about the problems they had. Can we go and see that?'

'We could take the road that passes it. I think it's rather boring, just a big green mound. You can run up and down, you can admire the view, but it insists on keeping all its secrets.' Dibby suddenly looked at Briar suspiciously. 'Did the stones tell *you* why it was built?'

'No.'

'No,' said Dibby, sounding relieved, 'they never do.'

'If I'd have told Mummy about the stones talking,' Briar confided as she snuggled up to Dibby, 'she'd have laughed at me. She'd have thought I was teasing. Daddy might believe, though. He says Freya showed him how to have listening ears.'

'It's harder when you're fully grown. Even my ears hear less well, and Mam says it's sad but I shall never be properly grown-up.'

'Freya says you are perfectly grown as you are, and Mary says you are delightfully dibby, and I think you are my very best aunt.'

'Do you really?' Dibb's face burst into bubble-beams of happiness. 'You really think I'm your very best aunt?'

'Yes,' Briar said, hugging Dibby Gran. 'Of course I do. We have so much in common, don't we? For I'm not exactly normal either, am I?'

'Why?' Dibby asked, her mouth all fly-gather gaping.

'Don't you remember? It took a drúkkerébema, a prophesy that had to be fulfilled, to make *me*, and I'm called Mega-brain at home . . . that's not normal!'

'I remember!' Dibby grinned, 'Mary's mother hen mum, Aunt Sally, wanted to help *your* mum so Great-gran was persuaded to start the drúkkerébema.'

'And I was the end.'

'Do you know, Briar, somehow I doubt that. A gift always has to be returned in one way or another. Great-gran taught us all that.'

'We could send postcards to Mummy and Daddy and Mam, to say thank you for letting us have our adventure.'

'Good idea,' Dibby agreed. 'We'll do it tomorrow, just before we leave.'

'Well, they seem happy enough,' Mary said, 'but for the life of me I can't remember saying your gran was delightfully dibby.'

'You probably said she was nutty as a fruit cake. Briar has had Aunt Emma to teach her – she was being polite.'

'Just as well,' Mary said. 'We don't want to upset Dibby now, do we?'

'Not ever,' I agreed, wondering where they'd send the cards.

It was mid-afternoon before we checked through the crystal again. Dibby and Briar had made good their camp. Bryony had been groomed until her coat shone, and was harnessed and ready to go.

'Don't forget the postcards!' Briar told Dibby, who promptly ordered Bryony to stand. 'One for Mummy, one for Daddy and one for Mam.'

'Mam can't read, but Tashar can. He could read it to her. We'll go to the shop opposite the pub. I think that one looks best.'

Dibby and Briar had to brush past a tall, scruffy youth loitering uneasily at the entrance. 'Excuse me, sir,' Dibby said politely in the gorgio-grovel way that sells baskets, pegs and flowers so well.

The gawky youth stepped backwards but he didn't answer. As they passed he turned his face abruptly away.

'He's what Freya would call a gutter gorgio,' Dibby whispered to Briar as they entered the tiny shop.

'That's not very polite, and stop doing that. Mummy says it's rude to hold your nose when someone stinks.'

'I didn't!' Dibby moved her hand quickly. 'I was scratching my nose.'

'No you weren't! Your nose was all screwed up, and so were your eyes.'

'I can't help that,' Dibby exclaimed. 'I bet he hasn't washed all over for at least a month.'

'Or possibly ever!'

The two of them giggled so much that the shop assistant had to cough twice before they heard her say. 'Can I help you?' They were still laughing as they flicked their way through the brightly coloured cards.

One postcard showed a man making baskets. Peeping out of a finished basket was a fluffy-faced kitten. Briar Rose crowed with glee. 'Kokko George once brought Mary a kitten like that. Can I send him a card too?'

'Another good idea,' Dibby said, and took the cards over to the counter lady. 'I'm Dibby,' Dibby explained, 'and I can't write, but I can remember the address. If I tell you, would you write it on the postcards for me, please? I don't mind paying extra.'

'It's very quiet today,' the lady smiled kindly at Dibby, 'so no trouble at all.'

'I can write!' Briar reminded Dibby proudly. 'I'm called Mega-brain.'

'But not quickly enough or small enough. I saw your letter to Freya. Your letters were mostly big and spiky, even I could see that, so we'll let the lady help us. When we make camp you can write and tell them all our news, and I shall make a lovely supper.'

'How will the lady know where to send them? Mummy and Daddy are moving somewhere. I haven't learned my new address yet.'

'Yes, even Mam will have probably moved.' Dibby looked at the pretty kitten postcard as she thought. 'I know! We'll send them *all* to Kokko George. He's a settled poshrat. He'll get them sorted for us. He'll pick up their patterans.'

The shop assistant found an envelope and popped the cards inside. 'Only have to write one address, then,' she explained. 'You can write more on the postcards, and just seal and post when you have finished.'

The shop lady was still handing the envelope to Briar when the scruffy youth burst into the shop, his woolly hat pulled over his face. He waved a large, shiny knife as he shouted, 'Give me the money!'

Instinctively, Dibby pushed Briar away from the man. Briar's eyes were wide in fear as she fell backwards and was lost in a pile of falling packages. 'I want my mummy! Mummy, help!' she screamed as china shattered all around her. Just for a moment the man lost concentration. Dibby took her chance and grabbed the long, glinting knife.

'That's *very* silly!' she told the startled youth firmly. 'And very rude. You have frightened my Briar, and that is very naughty indeed! If you want money you should ask nicely. Knives are for paring wood and slicing meat, not for waving at people. Mam says it is very dangerous to have knives near children, and Briar is a child. Do you hear me? Briar Rose is a child!'

The shop assistant shook her numbed brain back into activity. While the scruffy youth gawped in amazement at Dibby, she pressed an alarm button under the counter.

'I've called the police,' she told the cornered youth, 'so no more trouble.'

The lout no longer looked dangerous. His shoulders slumped and he began to look very scared indeed. 'You're mad!' he shouted as he shot past Dibby, who was lifting the knife high to make sure it was safe, but looked every bit as if she intended to split his skull in two.

'Not as mad as you!' Dibby yelled back, turning the knife towards him as she watched him flee towards the door of the shop. 'Threatening people is very wicked!' The boy didn't answer, he was too busy stumbling past unpacked stock boxes. 'You're so clumsy, a gavver will have no trouble catching you!' Dibby continued, still pointing the knife in the direction of his back as he fell over in his scramble to open the door.

'Gavver?'

'Policeman,' Dibby turned to the shop assistant to explain. 'A gavver is a policeman. Did you say they were on their way?'

The inept burglar took his chance to flee.

'Are you all right, Briar?'

Briar Rose tried to wipe black smudgy tears from her face as she nodded. 'I was frightened, Dibby. I was very scared.'

'You're quite safe with me,' Dibby said firmly. 'Haven't I always told you that? He was only a silly boy playing games.'

But Dibby looked very worried indeed as she pulled Briar up from the floor and nudged her towards the door. 'I'm sorry about the china, lady. Shall I pay for that too?'

The shop assistant stopped looking pasty-face white and smiled. 'No, of course not. You have saved my takings. The shop is insured. No it's *me* who has to thank you.'

'You wrote the postcards,' Dibby reminded her. 'Do you think I should find that silly gorgio and give him his knife?'

'I really did call the police. There's a button under the counter. Give it to them, that's best.'

Dibby's face fell. She remembered the police. They had accused her of stealing Briar, they had made her feel bad.

'You give them the knife,' she said. 'Briar has to be . . .' Dibby struggled to come up with an excuse and totally failed. Her hands clenched in frustration, her face flushed with the fear of losing Briar Rose, and of being locked up yet again.

Keep calm! I commanded Dibby through the crystal. 'Dibby, keep calm, you're doing really well! Just tell her you have to go!'

Dibby took a deep breath and her face flushed pink again. 'I have to look after Briar,' she explained, 'and we have to be somewhere else.'

'But . . .'

Dibby didn't wait to see what she wanted. She grabbed Briar Rose, who was still subdued with shock, and dragged her out of the shop. 'Quick . . . the vardo . . . we must hurry.'

Briar Rose made no attempt to argue. As soon as they were safe in the vardo, her colour returned and fear turned to elation. She didn't want to be forced to go home. The adventure with Dibby was far too exciting.

Dibby coaxed Bryony into her very fastest trot and headed into the side lane. By the time the police arrived at the shop, Dibby and Briar were long since gone. Mary and I shiver-sighed with relief. We felt very proud of Dibby. She *had* taken care of Briar. She had done really well.

18 'Mary, I know I must help'

The woman and the tree were both screaming! I heard them long before we turned the corner that allowed the fighting family to come into view.

A tall cherry tree stood trembling in terror in the front of a small but very neat garden. A small, thin woman clung to its trunk with all the tenacity of a hunting tiger, her lips curling as she snarled, 'It's mine! It's lovely! You can't cut it down, I won't let you!'

'It's only a tree, Shelley,' said the man she was shouting at, who was frothy-blood furious. Behind him two workmen sniggered uneasily.

'She can *hear* the tree screaming, Mary. I know I must help.'

'What nonsense! Trees can't scream. That woman's crazy to make so much fuss. The man's likely to blow a fuse any moment, and the two workmen look like gypsies . . . sorry, Freya . . . they look a bit on the dodgy side.'

I glower-glared. Mary had the decency to look shuffle-foot sheepish. 'You know I didn't mean any harm,' she said.

'They *are* gypsies,' I said, 'and they look fine to me.'

'How do you know?'

I didn't bother to answer. I was too busy. The woman and the tree had need of me. Together their voice was loud.

The two workmen said something to the man of the house. 'Wait,' he replied curtly. 'That tree is coming down today.'

The house was hug-foot close now. The woman's hysterical screams had brought the whole street out to watch. People peered from behind curtains, emptied endless things into dustbins and busily swept drives, anything to be able to get a better look.

I dismounted, took some heather from our carry bag, and then tied Domino to a lamppost. Mary treated

me to a really big glower-glare, before slipping off
Elsha and tethering her up too.

I looked all out-face confident as I walked up the
drive. The woman ignored me and continued to
scream. 'You can't cut down my beautiful tree.
Remember the glory of her pink blossoms in spring.
Look at the rich colours of her leaves. This tree has
lived quietly here for three generations. You can't cut
her down!'

I stood lizard-stone still and waited for someone
to notice me. If they did, they chose to do nothing.

'Shelley, be sensible! The concrete path is beginning to crack. The summer's been dry. Do you
really want subsidence? Do you really want our house
to tumble down round our ears after all we've done
to it?'

'It's too lovely to chop down!' The distraught
woman hugged her cherry tree trunk even harder. 'I
won't let you! I won't!'

'The walls will crack.'

'I don't care!'

'The house will lose value.'

'I don't care.'

'For God's sake, stop being so silly!' The man

162

grabbed the woman and tried to pull her from the tree. She screamed and clung limpet-tight. The tree whimpered in distress, its fear filled my mind, flooding me with misery.

The lady was right, it was a truly magnificent tree. It was such a shame to see it full of sadness, its leaves shimmering in distress, despair exuding from every pore. How sad it felt, knowing it was doomed to return to the earth. The woman, too, sensed the tree's tears. She clung even tighter, letting the tears mingle with her own. 'I won't let you die,' she promised. 'I won't!'

The two men with the chainsaw looked at each other impatiently. One moved, ready to give up and collect up his things.

'Stay!' the husband ordered.

The workmen looked uneasy. 'We don't want any trouble, mister. We can come back tomorrow . . . or when you get this sorted.'

'I said stay!'

I edged forward, watched by a million curious eyes. People weren't even pretending to go about their usual business.

'Don't get involved!' Mary warned.

'I have to. The tree and the woman are calling me.'

I had to do something and I had to do it now. I marched straight up to the angry man and thrust my heather into his hand. 'Buy the lady some lucky heather, it will change your fortune.'

'Oh, for heaven's sake!'

'Lucky heather for the lady?'

The man scowled but he made no attempt to push me away. I felt no fear, not because I was stupid, but because the workmen *were* gypsies, so it was impossible for me to come to much harm.

For a long moment nothing happened. It was like time was frozen. The woman clung to the tree, her arms grubby from so much hugging. I continued to offer my lucky heather. Mary looked worried, and the workmen leaned idly against the silent saw. Brooms rested in hands, curtains failed to flutter, neighbours stood rooted to the spot in their little drives.

'I think we should leave it for now, squire?'

'Well I don't! Enough time has been wasted already.'

I seemed to be the least of the man's problems, so he decided to sort me out first. He dug his hands into

164

his pocket and pulled out fifty pence. 'That's your lucky heather money, gypsy. Now, GO!'

I held my heather close to the man but I didn't let go. 'Let me give it to the lady, sir. Let me bring you both some luck.'

'Lucky heather won't help *me*,' the man said, sounding more resigned than cross. 'I'll save her blooming house and get hung for it.'

The lady of the house didn't seem to care about her home. She yelled,'I won't let him murder my beautiful tree!'

'If you cut the top back hard,' I told the man, 'it won't need to grow very long roots. If you pollard the tree it won't need to drink so much water and the house will be safe.'

'It's too late for that! Look, gypsy, the concrete has deep cracks already. She should have let me cut the top back when I first suggested it years ago.'

'Freya!' Mary called anxiously from her place near the gate. 'Come back! Please!'

'It's all right, Mary,' I hissed. 'Just keep the hosses calm.'

I inspected the path that ran along the edge of the carefully maintained little house. The man was right to be concerned. The damage from the tree was already severe. It *was* too big and too close. It rose out of the patchy hedge on the other side of the handkerchief lawn, like a copper-coloured giant. It was shiver-spine splendid to look at, but it had feet strong as steel, and its arms stole so much light that little else would grow.

'I will tell you what to do,' I told the man.

'Cheeky minx!' one of the gypsies said to the other, but I could tell his tone was admiring.

'Got to be a Boswell or a Loveridge,' the other replied. 'Those women are born with no nerves at all.'

'And how much will your advice cost?' the man asked suspiciously, willing to listen now his lady was showing an interest and growing more calm.

'Nothing. I will help because I want to.'

'Not a normal gypsy, then?' the man muttered, and the Romanies behind him nodded agreement and laughed.

I went up to the beautiful coppery cherry and wrapped my arms round its trunk too. 'I will help you,' I whispered. The woman said nothing but her eyes watched every move I made.

I offered the lady the lucky white heather, and while she fidget-fingered the delicate, dried flower heads, I spoke quietly to the doomed cherry. When we had finished our talk time, I took the lady's hand and led her gently away.

'The tree realises that it is hurting your house,' I told the lady. 'The tree says she is sorry, but even so she does not wish to die. The tree says she is happy, however, to become a hedge.'

'What?'

'The tree spirits say they can recover. They say that if you stick some branches deep into the earth, they will grow. There are plenty of gaps in your hedge, after all. The tree says if you keep her well watered and trim her back carefully when she grows, you will have the most beautiful hedge in the whole of the street in no time, and she will live again.'

'Tree spirit?' the woman said. 'You spoke to the tree spirit?'

'The tree is a living thing, *you* know that. That's why you were so sad that it has to die. Trees have a heart spirit, as does everything that lives. The tree says that if you take care of her, she will do her very best to give you pleasure. She will reward you with

167

the brightest leaves, the sweetest fruits, and the most glorious flowers. The tree says she can be happy as a hedge. Birds can still nest in her, the wind can still comb her hair. She says it is worth a little pain so everyone can be happy.'

'Will a hedge really grow?'

'Every branch will become a bush. From death comes life, it is the way of the world, but she asks one thing.'

'What?'

'While she is felled we must cover our ears. She does not want to scare us with her screams.'

The woman looked at her house, she looked at her tree, her husband and the men with the saw. Finally her eyes turned back to me. She nodded.

'You can cut her down now,' I told the men, who plugged their ears and turned on the giant humming saw. I couldn't help but giggle-grin. The gorgios thought the Romanies were saving their ears from the decibel saw noises, but I knew better. They were blocking their ears from the screams of the wounded tree, who wished, like all trees, to be allowed to die with dignity.

The woman and I, fingers in our ears, watched

silently with Mary and the man. The copper giant slowly shrank, branches were hacked away and piled up round her feet. The tree groaned in protest, dark sounds that vibrated in my bones. I stuffed my fingers so hard that my ears shared her pain.

The man and Mary shared uneasy shrugs. The gypsies worked until their bodies shone with sweat. They kept their eyes lowered and didn't speak or smile. Slowly, the tree died. Soon, there was only a stark trunk to remind us of her glory. The lady of the house stood silently with me, tears rolling down her cheeks, her ears still muffled from the whining saw sounds.

At last it was done. I rushed over to stroke the silent branches. The men left to quench their thirst before fetching a trailer to take the tree corpse away.

The lady watched me as I chose nine firm long branches that were not to thick or too thin, too young or too old. I sent Mary for my knife, and then cut all the side branches away, leaving just a few leaves at the top. I finally trimmed the ground edge to a triangle just below a bud, to ease its way deep into the soil.

'Like this,' I said, plunging the first strike deep into the earth, so that far more lay buried than above.

'Will you . . .'

'No, the rest have to be planted by you. The tree spirit has to know from the very first you are fighting to give her life. You plant them. Mary and I will make sure you do it well.'

The lady of the house planted a near naked branch in every gap in the hedge. She planted all nine. When she had finished her face was calm and smiling. 'They *will* grow,' she said confidently. 'They will grow for *me.*'

'Yes, but they will stay silent all summer. Water them well, for they must not be allowed to become dry. This is not the best time for a new beginning. Tell them each day that you care, that you are longing to see their first new buds of life. If you are lucky, you may see signs before winter, but if not, do not worry. Tell them even if it snows. There *will* be growth in spring. The tree has chosen to live; you must not doubt.'

I took back my lucky heather and gave her the fifty pence. 'You don't need the heather, but I do. There will be other gorgios in need of help.'

'Thank you so much.' The lady's face was still wet with tears but she was smiling. She did not notice that her man now stood behind her, winking at me from over her shoulder. Happy now all was calm.

'My pleasure, missus,' I said, using my best gorgio-greeting voice, 'and good luck stay with you and your pink cherry hedge.'

I winked at the Roms who were packing up ready to go as I left. 'Boswell!' I said. 'I'm a Boswell.'

'Had to be,' said one.

'Remember me to Mam,' said the other. 'Joseph Loveridge, tell her, Joseph Loveridge. Knew her before you were even a twinkle.'

While the lady of the house had gone to fetch water, her husband reached out to shake my hand. 'Take this,' he said gruffly. 'You earned every penny.'

I smiled happily as we mounted the horses. We were twenty pounds richer. If we were careful we could live on that for days.

'Will it really grow?' Mary asked as soon as we had ridden far enough away.

'I think so, it has a good chance,' I told her. 'But I am curious about one thing. I wonder if she will tell her man about the sticks she has planted or whether she will button her lip until pink-petal flowers waken his memory one cherry-happy spring.'

19 Wayland's Smithy

The Uffington White Horse seemed to dance lightly over the downs as we climbed up the hill that led from the road to the Ridgeway. Mary stopped frequently to stare in admiration.

'I wonder if Dad has seen him? It's amazing. Such simple lines cut into the chalk making something so wonderfully fluid.'

'He wouldn't look right painted on the playroom wall,' I told Mary. 'He belongs here, commanding the rolling hills of Berkshire.'

'Why here?'

'It is said,' I told Mary, using my let-me-tell-you-a-tale voice, 'that Wayland the blacksmith once owned

172

a white horse. It was fast and elegant and extremely loyal, in fact the most beautiful horse in the world. The people sacrificed him, burying him deep in the soil, so he could keep Berkshire eternally beautiful. Those chalkland cuts on the hill are there to remind us of him for ever.

'As soon as the horse had been slain and the people saw how Wayland the blacksmith mourned for his lovely white mare, they felt sorry for him and wished to give him back something of what he had lost. They went to the Blowing Stone near Kingston Lisle, just over the hill from here. They blew through the holes at midnight and summoned the great panther, Pahn, who is, as you know, the guardian of the night.

'The people stayed at the stone blowing for help until they smelled a sweetness in the air that they knew was the breath of Pahn. They were shiver-spine scared, for they knew that that same sweetness could lure them into becoming prey. They locked up their fear and waited, because until Wayland the smithy smiled not a shoe could be shod, for often he could not see for tears.

'The great panther Pahn was impressed with their braveness. He was even more touched by the tears

Wayland shed for his horse, so he agreed that Berkshire could stay beautiful for as long as the people had it in their hearts to care. He gently licked the salty tears from Wayland's eyes and told him that at night, under his protection, the Uffington White Horse could rise again. From dusk until dawn the horse and Wayland are free to roam as they please. The beautiful hills of Berkshire belong to them.

'It is said that, because of this, Wayland the smith will live for ever; that sometimes, when the moon shines silver soft, you can see him endlessly wandering the Ridgeway, talking to the horse he cannot bear to leave.'

'Oh, what rubbish, Freya!'

'You wait and see!'

She pushed me hard. I nearly fell off Domino, who reared in surprise. 'You wait and see,' I laughed, as I pushed her back. Happily, we headed west along the Icknield Way, towards the long barrow named Wayland's Smithy.

'How can you be sure Dibby will be here?'

'The horses need to be shod, and Dibby will know that Briar would love to see how she does it.'

'Dibby's a blacksmith now? No, don't tell

me! You're going to ask Wayland?'

'Not exactly,' I admitted, failing to smother a smirk.

'The middle of nowhere is an odd place for a forge.' Mary gazed down the long and narrow lane that seemed to travel incessantly over the gentle swelling hills. She looked at me suspiciously. 'This is a place for hikers in leather boots and strange butterfly hunters. Come dusk, the back-packers will be pubbing and the place will be even more deserted. It's the very last place you want a smithy! So what on earth do you think will happen?'

I giggle-grinned. 'That's for me to know and you to find out, but don't forget, once, long ago, this was the major road.'

'Oh! Mystery time again, is it?' Mary said, pretending she wasn't the least bit interested. 'Well, at least we'll have some time with Dibby and Briar.'

We rode for almost a mile along the chalky lane before we spotted Dibby and Briar chasing round the ancient burial mound at high speed, hooting with laughter.

'Is *this* Wayland's Smithy?' Mary asked, her mouth dropping. 'You really meant the actual long barrow! I was expecting a forge somewhere close by. Dibby and Briar shouldn't play chase on burial grounds, we better stop them.'

'The dead here are either gone to the happy place where Great-gran *should* be, or else doomed to walk the hills,' I told Mary firmly. 'Either way, they will not worry about innocents like Dibby and Briar. The tombs are empty, they'll come to no harm.'

'It doesn't seem right.'

'Nor does living for ever,' I said, feeling sorry for the Wayland smith, who could not face leaving his favourite horse.

Briar spotted us and pointed. The two cackling girls abandoned their game and raced to meet us. 'Has Bryony been shod?' I asked, when all the hugs and kisses that Briar and Mary demanded were over.

'No, I *knew* you would come.' Dibby led Elsha and Domino over to Bryony and fed them carrots fetched from my vardo. 'They can all be done together.'

I nodded.

'Freya, let me keep the vardo tonight. It's my journey. I'll cook for us all . . . I'll do anything,' Dibby pleaded.

Mary looked at my lovely, cosy wagon. She

opened her mouth ready to plead for a nice comfy bed, but I knuckle-nudged her firmly. 'It's your adventure,' I told Dibby as Mary forced a smile. 'Of course you shall have the wagon.'

'I'll make us supper,' Dibby said happily. 'I'll make everyone supper.'

'Oh, good!' Mary whispered to me sarcastically. 'Another rabbit stew.'

'I'll make something different,' Dibby said quickly, determined to stay in charge. She washed her hands and put on her white cooking pinny.

'Dibbs, we've plenty of fresh bread, it's lovely and crusty. Could you create a really speciall bowie-zoomi?'

'Yes, soup is easy,' Dibby agreed. 'You gather the herbs and I'll sort out the rest.'

'Must we?'

'Oh, come on, Mary. I'll pick the herbs and you will have the chance to chat with Briar and make sure she's gorgio-girl happy. You don't mind if Briar comes for a walk, do you, Dibbs?'

'You could tell her about the horse. She thinks it's a dragon. I was going to tell her, but the dragon was much more fun. It chased me all round the smithy.'

It was late in the day when we returned with chickweed, plus marjoram, lemon balm and borage, all pinched from a cottage garden,

'Will this do? There's not much to find here.'

Dibby nodded happily. Briar greeted her with a kiss and wanted to help with the cooking. Mary looked worried. I grabbed her and pulled her towards the trees. 'Come *on*, Mary. She might be daft but she's not stupid. Briar is well guarded. Come, let's find more wood for the fire.'

The bowie-zoomi was warm-soul wonderful. We hacked off chunks of fresh bread, piled them with butter and ate them with our soup. We stuffed ourselves full-tummy fat and felt happy-heart light. 'You cook really well,' Mary admitted, licking her fingers. 'That was a real treat. What was it?'

I nudged Dibby, but she didn't understand, her head was stuffed full of pride.

'Thank you,' she said. 'It is my favourite soup too. It's called bowie-zoomi and it is made from snails.'

'Snails!' Mary shrieked. 'I thought it was chicken.' Her face washed over all sea-sick green as she rushed over to the hedge to throw up.

Dibby looked confused, hurt and angry, all at the very same time. Briar made the mistake of hooting with laughter, and Dibbs rushed into the vardo in floods of tears. Briar tried to follow, but Dibbs slammed the door fast shut and absolutely refused to be comforted.

'For goodness sake, Mary! Just look what you've done.'

'It was snails,' Mary wailed, pouring half of our water over her face. 'You never told me it was *snails*!'

'You told me that snails were a luxury. It was definitely you told me that, and, anyway, they tasted good, didn't they?'

'That's in France! I'm not French! The snails were nice, but they were only nice before I knew. After that they turned my stomach! I'm sorry I upset Dibbs, but I can't eat snails. They're slimy and horrid.'

'That's slugs!' I explained, not even trying to smother giggle grins. 'Some Romany folk don't eat snails though.'

'Some have got some sense then?'

'Not really, they just feel that snails are like us, committed to travel through life with their homes on their backs. However, most of us think they're delicious. Churen is very fond of snails, they're his favourite.'

'Don't be silly! Churen wouldn't eat snails.'

'Churen is a proper Romany so bowie-zoomi is a treat,' I told her. 'If you don't believe me, ask him.'

'Oh, I will!' Mary said. 'I certainly will.'

It took Mary a long time to make friends with Dibby. Gorgio white lies sprouted like seeds. 'The soup was wonderful. I'm so sorry I was sick. It was the horse-riding that made me ill, or else I must have eaten a funny plant when we were gathering herbs, and Briar wasn't laughing at *you*, she was laughing at me.'

I nodded agreement. That bit at least was true.

'Shall we shoe the horses tonight?' Dibby asked, mollified by Mary's attempts at simpering sweetness.

I nodded. 'If the horses are ready we can move on tomorrow. I will show Mary the Blowing Stone and that will give you and Briar a chance to get ahead. We'll meet up again at Rollright.'

'Why can't we go together?' Mary asked. 'Mam wants us to, and now we are together . . .'

'Dibby needs to take Briar full circle *alone*,' I insisted, making my voice loud so Dibby, who was looking stop-heartbeat worried, could be sure we wouldn't spoil things. 'You and I have better fish to fry.'

'What fish?'

'Churen,' I said, winking at Dibby and Briar.

'Well, perhaps it wouldn't hurt,' Mary agreed, scowling when Dibby asked if she fancied him.

We chatted until midnight, when we tethered the horses close to the great, oblong granites that edged the entrance to the tomb. We placed three silver coins on the top of a flat stone to the right, one for each horse, before going inside.

'Do we have to wait in here?' Mary asked. Scaling houses meant nothing to her, but she found sitting in long-ago tombs shake-limb scary.

'What will we see?' asked Briar. 'Will we have to wait long?'

'You will need the crystal to see,' I told Mary and Briar. 'I do not need it, and neither does Dibby. The images you see will be bright in our minds too.'

Mary sat cuddle-close to Briar, who showed no hint of fear. The linking crystal rested in her lap. Dibby and I waited for the moon to grow curious and peep inside our tomb. When the morning hour reached three, usually the quietest time of all, the light lit our crystal, which began to glow.

To the left of our tomb appeared a stocky man on a pure white horse. He rode her gently, talking quietly to her. She was responding with lightly flicking ears. When he reached the tomb portal he stroked her neck delicately with his fingers as he waited. His hands held the power of a blacksmith but his touch was light as gossamer. The white horse whinnied softly, and the muscles of her neck shimmied with pleasure.

To the right appeared a wagon . . . Churen's vardo dressed glittering gold and emerald green. Wayland the smith smiled and waved. Churen dismounted. The two horses nuzzled gently, black to white, each one perfect.

'Busy night,' Churen stated, adding his silver to ours before helping Wayland check the hooves of all the horses. 'Let me help.'

He lit a fire close to the left side of the long barrow. It didn't matter that we were inside. The earth mound behaved as if transparent. There was magic enough to let all of us see.

Wayland fished in his saddlebag for irons and bellows. The two men worked easily together, a practice born of time. The flames danced deep-heat blue. The arched shoes on the anvil glowed fiery red, and were perfectly formed to fit the hoof for which they were made. One by one the horses were shod, and only when every one was done did Wayland take his silver coins and prepare to leave.

'Will you take my wagon for a while?' Churen asked.

Wayland nodded. 'You are called to watch tonight, then? You are lucky, though. Most of the time you are free.'

Churen patted the rump of his great black Shire. 'I am not free any more,' he told Wayland. 'I was once, but now someone has captured my heart.'

Wayland the smith smiled as he tethered his precious mare to Churen's wagon. 'Then you are like me,' he said, 'doomed to be a willing prisoner for ever.'

'Yes, but not yet,' Churen said, and in that moment he was gone. An owl hooted from the branch of an overhanging tree. Wayland smiled, waved and rode into his endless night.

'What did you feed those snails on?' Mary asked Dibby to release the magic. 'I've never shared a dream before.'

'No dream,' Dibby said, as we all scrambled outside to stretch our legs and breathe in cool fresh air. 'Look at the horses! Dreams are only in your head.'

Mary and Briar checked each horse in turn. They were all freshly shod. The silver coins were nowhere to be seen. Still not satisfied, they inspected the earth around the barrow. Eventually they gave up, for the sandman called loudly to them.

'What on earth were they doing?' Dibby asked, harnessing Bryony as soon as Briar had tucked herself up in the vardo.

'They were looking for warm ashes and old metal shoes.'

Dibby laughed. 'Gorgios are funny! Did they really think they'd find them?'

I looked at Mary, tucked up asleep in the bender oblivious to the fresh taste of dawn. I nodded. 'To a gorgio a ghost is not normal unless it's fudged in mist or wrapped in sheets, maybe even carrying a severed head.'

Dibby snorted, she was still giggling as she walked Bryony and my vardo away.

20 'Do you think Churen will come back soon?'

'Do you think Churen will come back soon?' Mary asked sadly, as we plodded the long trek back home. 'Can we do the acorn cup and ash tree key magic again?'

'No! I told you, only once. He came, so you know one of us will be his wife one day. Surely that is enough. He is no puppet to dance to our strings. When he is ready, he will come.'

'Are you sure?' Mary asked the next day and the next, and just when I was getting wrinkle-brow irritable, he came.

We woke at dawn to find his wagon stood close to our bender. I, who would normally wake at the whinny of a distant mare, had not heard a single thing.

Mary spotted him first. She had had to leave the bender, woken by the need to relieve herself from an excess of Earl Grey tea. She rushed back in to give me the news.

'And I've no lipstick!' she screeched. 'No perfume, nothing.'

'You don't need them,' I told her. 'You are pretty enough.'

'No,' Mary said suspiciously, 'you just want to be prettier!'

'Sometimes you can really be cruel,' I told Mary crossly and, because I was fluffy-fur furious, I brushed my hair until it shone like black satin, which Mary thought Churen liked better than red-fire bold. 'All's fair in love or war!'

'I don't care!' Mary retorted, but her poky-nose nature made her more calm when she spotted me shredding herbs. 'What on earth are you doing now?'

'Sprinkling borage leaves in my washing water,' I said. 'Didn't you know that borage leaves always attract a man?'

I felt a curious mix of laughter and anger as Mary snatched away my bowl, my *personal* washing-bowl that Tashar, my brother, had made just for me. She dowsed her head in the bowl. I half expected it to wedge round her ears. Every bit of her brilliant red hair was stuck with shredded flakes of borage.

'You'll not get the better of me, Freya Boswell, you should know that!'

I shrugged, all out-face casual. With Great-gran to help me I felt I didn't need to net Churen at all!

Despite our quarrel we made the best of the day. The sun shone and we all went fishing. It was warm-ways wonderful.

'I thought we'd be riding off after Dibby and Briar,' Churen teased, as we sat idly on the bank enjoying ourselves. 'I thought it was most important that you found her, and here we are busily wasting time.'

'Rainbow trout for supper will be a nice change. Even venison gets long-time boring.' I threw my line into the sluggish river. 'And, anyway, a day by water always eases the mind.'

'But you were so worried about Briar . . . well Mary was,' Churen pulled out his hook as he spotted ripples dancing on the water, scowled and threw it back again. He was being a muddle-minded fisherman. I wondered if he did better at night when he could turn into a heron. I suspected he wasn't the least bit interested in fish; it was us he was drawing in.

'Briar is fine,' Mary told him firmly, as she pretended that fishing was the most exciting thing she had ever done. 'Dibby is caring for Briar really well.'

'How do you know?'

'We check through . . .'

I glared at Mary. Churen might be one of us, but she had no right to tell him the secrets of our linking crystal. Mary saw sense enough to button her lip.

'. . . through Freya's strange gypsy ways. We follow patterans, and Freya . . . feels . . .'

'You've caught a fish!' I said, pleased to interrupt.

Mary went pasty-white pale. It was obvious she had no idea how to reel in her catch. Churen winked at me. My heart skylark-soared, but I just smiled and let him show her the way.

They never noticed when I slipped back to the bender . . . well Mary noticed, but gave not a hint at all.

There wasn't much time to set up this magic. They would soon get hollow-belly hungry. We had not eaten all day.

I searched round for the materials I needed. I was lucky that Briar had played in our bender. She had left it filled with paper and crayons.

I had wanted to use photographs because the faces are so much clearer, but as I had none of those, I set to with paper and did my very best to draw like Mary's dad had once shown me.

Drawing Mary was easy. How many girls are there with cornflower-blue eyes and hot-fire hair? I made her nose pertly pointed, added some freckles, and I was done.

Churen took more time. Moody eyes are clench-fist hard to put on paper, and how do you draw a casual smile that is only just there? I did the very best I could. I nearly bit off my tongue with trying but, I have to say, he wasn't the man in my heart. I crayoned his clothes charcoal black and used Briar's best red pen to strike his belt scarlet and bold.

'What are you doing?' Mary asked, poky-nose curious as to why I had gone missing so long. I stuffed my drawings down my smock to hide them away.

189

'Nothing.'

'A bigger bosom won't help you,' Mary said. 'He must know by now you have almost nothing at all.'

'I've served the fish!' Churen called, saving me from my tickling tongue. 'Come and eat before it gets cold.'

Dinner was tingle-lip tasty. We stuffed ourselves silly and grew close again by the evening fire.

'I could stay like this for ever,' Mary whispered, and I knew she longed to reach out for Churen's hand.

'Ever is a long time,' Churen said. 'I should know.'

'You can be as silly as Freya,' Mary teased. Churen took no offence. His eyes twinkled in wicked delight.

'So you think it is silly to drift endlessly on for ever, called when you are needed by night to dance for the stones?'

'It sounds exciting,' I said, curious to know how he felt in his inner depths.

'It's only exciting sometimes,' Churen fished a small bone out from between his teeth. 'Mostly it's like being in limbo, waiting in a land of dreams.'

'Oh, here we go again! Have you got shares with the sandman?'

'Perhaps I *am* the sandman.'

'Oh, for goodness sake!' Mary said, only just hanging on to her sense of humour. 'Is there no sense in you at all?'

'If I choose to marry you,' Churen said, looking her straight in the eye. 'I suppose I would have to become perfectly normal and perfectly boring.'

'No you don't!' Mary threw a hand towel at Churen. 'Just because you would have to taste reality, doesn't mean you'd have to give up on your silly dreams.'

'Can I share your night trances?' I asked Churen, more to annoy Mary than to show I believed.

'We can always share dreams,' Churen said softly, 'whatever happens.'

I realised that in that moment the truth washed over him. If I chose to take my own path I would not be totally alone. We could still share the misty-magic world of visions, for one or other of us would be the voice of Pahn.

'If you choose Mary,' I said, feeling a creep-bit better, 'you would still have eternity, not through your own bones, but through those of your children, and your children's children.'

191

'Would you like to have children with me?' Churen teased Mary, wide-mouth-open laughing when he saw how she blushed.

Later, when the evening was long past and the others slept, I rose to finish the picture magic.

In Mary's bag I found her small cosmetic mirror. I placed her carefully crayoned picture behind it, and stuck Churen's in front so they rested nose to nose. I pulled from my carry bag some more of the red silk that I had long ago stolen from Churen. I carefully wrapped up Mary's mirror, with its nose to nose paintings, and secured the cummerbund parcel with neatly knotted strands. Satisfied my parcel was secure, I crept out of our bender and into Churen's wagon.

He slept like a time-worn baby, his body draped across feather-soft pillows. Even though the door clicked, he failed to stir. I wondered if in his dreams he was still with us, or if he roamed mazes, woods and rivers in an eternal wait to be summoned by stone.

I took a long look at the man I loved so much yet did not want to be mine, except in dreams. I locked away the doubts that still lingered and hid Mary's mirror in a small crevice at the back of the shelf that stood over his head.

Mirror lost
Mirror found
Be they magic linked
And magic bound.

I could not make Churen choose Mary, indeed I had no wish for that. Man has been designed by nature for the hunt. But I could ensure that thoughts of her would fill his mind, at least until the mirror was shattered, or lost in time. I had to make sure that no matter what Great-gran planned, he wouldn't snare me.

21 'The circle was almost closed'

We were nearing Rollright Stones. The circle was almost closed.

Mary rode well now. As a treat I had given her Domino and taken Elsha as my mount, yet she rode ridged-face sullen.

'What's wrong?'

'I suppose Churen will be yours! I suppose I shall have to go back to school and this holiday will feel like it's never been.'

'Holiday romances are normal,' I heckled. 'You're not grown-up until you've had one.'

'Not when your best friend is a Romany, with nothing to stop her stealing your man away.'

'Why should I make him mine?' I wore my best tickle-tease voice. The one Aunt Emma had taught me so many years ago. Mary was too sad to notice.

'Tell me you don't love him.'

'I can't' I told her open-heart honestly. 'I'll love him for ever and ever, but he can never be mine . . . except in a land of dreams.'

'Why?'

'I am a chime child. If I take him I lose everything.'

'Oh, what rubbish!' Mary said. 'The magic won't vanish just because you get married.'

I felt shiver-sad. She was probably right. After all, the herbs and their powers were still the same. 'It's a matter of belief,' I told her sadly. 'As far as my people are concerned, I am a chime child, so marriage cannot be for me, and anyway, if I took me a life mate, then he would take from me too. There would not be the time to work the magic well.'

'How can I be sure you won't steal him?' Mary asked. 'If you really loved him, you'd be ready to give everything up. Family, friends, *everything.*'

'No, you are wrong,' I told her. 'I have thought and decided. My people, even your people, need a choviar now, and that is me.' I crossed my fingers behind my back. Where was Great-gran? I knew I was being open-heart honest; producing the greatest choviar in the whole world was too great a sacrifice to ask, for it meant the loss of the life work that had become me.

Mary did not believe me. Great-gran thought differently too. She had plotted so hard for Churen and me to be joined, but I knew what was wanted now. My people, living people, had need of me. I knew I must walk away, but nothing was certain. It was still *her* fingers that licked the stones in restless blue.

'You don't marry your people, Freya. You choose the man, not the family!'

'*You* don't, Mary . . . we *do*. The one is the same as the other.'

She still looked dull-face miserable, so I decided it was time to give her a present. I dug into my carry bag and pulled out the necklace that I had made before I had set my feet free.

I had threaded acorns and sunflower seeds alternately on a thread of Churen's fine red silk. It had taken ages to make, for the sunflower seeds were small and brittle with a tendency to split, even though the thread was eye-of-a-needle fine.

'An acorn necklace!' Mary said not the least impressed. 'Just what I always wanted . . . I don't think!'

'You'll want this one,' I told her. 'It's a love magnet. The red ribbon will bring fertility when the time is right. I took it from Churen's belt. The acorns are Mother Nature's best beginning, and the sunflower seeds will draw him to you as a flower to the sun.'

Mary stopped being worry-worded and giggled. 'Oh, Freya! When will you ever stop having such strange ideas? It's impossible to stay cross with you for long.'

I put the necklace I had never worn around her neck, trying desperately to subdue the demons that scratched at my heart. 'You don't have to wear my silly magic.'

'Oh but, Freya,' Mary admitted, making sure the necklace was safely placed. 'I do!'

22 'Churen chooses. You promised!'

Dibby sang out loud as she drove my vardo with its bright green roof, red and gold sides and bright yellow wheels up the steep hill that led back to Rollright Stones.

'Full circle,' she trilled happily. 'I am back at my birthplace and I have walked through fire.'

'You were born here?'

'Yes, I was birthed right in the centre of the king's men. Great-gran says they represent ordinary people, so she decreed it so.'

'It's a funny place to be born,' Briar said, looking at the the small circle screened by a few simple trees.

'It wasn't always like this. Once the stones were

in the middle of a forest, well hidden from the gorgio world. Later, when the forest was gone, five larches were planted, right in the circle.'

'Why?'

'To protect the stones from the wind. But the roots grew too big, and if the larches blew down, the stones could be hurt, so they were cut down soon after I was born. We took some stems though, and planted them in the lane, so the trees had life again.'

Dibby took Briar's hand and led her gently round the ring, touching each stone in turn. 'If I hadn't been head-banged silly, *I* would have been the greatest choviar of all, and Freya would not have been born.'

'Is that right?' Mary asked, as we watched them through the crystal.

'Yes, Rollright is her birth circle. It is there she will enter and leave the spirit world. Everyone should have a birth circle, even if it's only marked with little white stones. Everyone should be born in touch with the earth.'

'Where's yours, then?'

'That's for me to know and you to guess,' I told Mary, 'but if I took Churen, then the new choviar would be born in the very same place.'

'*Churen chooses*!' Mary grabbed my shoulders so suddenly that the crystal fell out of her lap and rolled away. 'Churen chooses. YOU PROMISED!'

'OK, when Churen chooses, when fire meets water, sun meets moon, sky meets earth . . .'

Mary let me go as suddenly as she had grabbed me. I rescued the crystal which had tumbled into a hollow further down the bank.

'I love him,' Mary said, looking lost-soul sad. 'I don't think he's practical, I don't even think he's clever. He'd probably be no good at all in the gorgio world, but I do love him.'

'You're a school girl,' I said, using my best Aunt Emma teasing voice.

'It makes no difference,' Mary whispered softly. 'Common sense has nothing to do with this. I don't mind waiting nine years, I'd wait for ever.'

'Ever is a very long time.'

'I hate you, Freya Boswell! Sometimes I really *hate* you!'

This time there were no gentle pushes, for now she meant every word.

'Watch the crystal, Mary. Dibby and Briar have entered the circle. They are almost home.'

Mary settled herself beside me. 'I do hate you,' she said, 'but I love you too.'

I nodded. Sometimes I felt like that about Ostrich Gran, and Dibby felt like that every time Mam said, 'Do take care' or 'It's too dangerous for you to try'. All of us are bound by the ribbons of love.

'We have come full circle,' Dibby and Briar sang. 'We have taken care and walked through the fire.'

'Look at that, Freya,' exclaimed Mary. 'The stones are *dancing*, and would you believe it, each stone has the face of a watching cat.'

My chest felt puff-ball bursting with pride. A gorgio would have seen nothing but a woman and child dancing. A gorgio would have presumed them made momentarily mad by the fullness of the moon. The blood of Kokko George had stirred at last in her veins.

In the centre of the swaying stones Dibby and Briar hooted with the joy that only Bastet could bring. Slowly and gracefully the stones moved backwards and forwards, to the left and then to the right, all perfectly in tune with the strange music that filled our hearts until we could bubble-burst with happiness.

'I looked after Briar,' Dibby sang. 'I can't be that stupid because I did it all by myself.'

'Dibby and I had a proper adventure,' Briar sang to the stones. 'I learned I didn't need a sticky-brick house. I learned Dibby is wonderful. I learned to be me.'

The haunting melody grew even louder. The stones moved as if holding hands. They slowly circled the simple-souled lady and the gifted young child.

'I learned I am Dibby,' Dibby trilled happily, 'and I learned it is good to be me.'

'I know that music,' Mary whispered. 'Only Churen can fill the air with such a lovely sound. Not even your brother Vashti can give dance to stones.'

'Great-gran needed the music to refresh Dibby's soul,' I told Mary as we watched Dibby and Briar walk round the stones, touching them gently one by one.

'What are they doing? They look mad as hatters . . . both of them.'

'They're thanking their stone circle friends, telling them that their work is done, their journey is safely over. Dibby and Briar have shared a real adventure. Briar has learned a little about magic, about how to follow your dreams, and Dibby, well just look at Dibby, she's really *alive*!'

Slowly the music faded and the stones stood as they always had, silently upon a windswept hill. 'Thank you again!' Dibby called out as they turned to walk away. 'I am a real, grown-up person now. I can't wait to tell Mam.'

'Will Mam let her go?'

'Dibby won't let herself be bossed about now,' I said, 'and Mam will know there is no need. She can survive and be happy, and that is clever enough!'

I waited for Mary to argue, to tell me that nothing had really changed, that Dibby was still a child wrapped up in middle years, sugar sweet and soap-bubble soft in the head, but she didn't, she just stared into the crystal looking slightly sad. 'Our Dibbys are kept on leads too,' she said, 'even tighter ones and, unlike Dibby, they'll never be free to walk through the fire.'

23 Rollright red ribbon

'I wonder if I shall have to spend the rest of my life being summoned by stones?' Mary muttered. She was feeling yawn-gape weary of travelling. If it hadn't been for Churen, she would have long ago gone home.

'You'll miss us when you're safe back in your gorgio world, especially Churen.' My soft-silly centre felt sad. All these years, Mary and I had been more glue-stuck than sisters, but now, suddenly, Churen held more of her heart than me.

Mary scowled. 'I might just as well go. What chance have I of marrying Churen? Your great-gran wants the greatest witch of all time to succeed her, and it looks like it isn't you.'

I nodded sadly. Great-gran had gone to a bigger place, grown bigger dreams. Her plot plans were minding more to the future. All the magic in heaven hadn't turned Ostrich Gran into an angel, and if it did, she wouldn't seem as much fun to me.

'I might as well go now!'

'Stay!'

Mary shrugged. She felt tear-drop ocean sad despite looking outside-easy. I longed to give her a hug to show her how much I cared, but the time was not right, there could be no gorgio grizzles now.

We waited together in an uneasy silence, watching the fingers of the night lick at the patiently waiting stones.

Churen chose normality as a chariot. He came not as flying fish or leaping bear, he did not metamorphose from shadow. This time his green and gold wagon drove sedately across the brown, furrowed field accompanied by the sound of shaking wheels and the gentle snorts of the giant black Shire.

'Great-gran has chosen now for her time,' Churen said, offering us both his easy smile, 'so tonight should be fun, shouldn't it?'

'I doubt it!' Mary said sourly. 'As far as I can

see, Great-gran's middle name is trouble.'

'No,' Churen said. 'Great-gran always means well, and she's usually right.'

'So, what makes the old Ostrich's schemes so special for you?' I teased. 'What magic moment is this when you have all the time in the world? A whole eternity of falling in with poky-prod plans.'

'I want to hate her,' Mary sighed, 'but I can't. Life for Ostrich Gran is like a huge game of chess . . . and I was dealt to be a pawn.'

'Oh, we all feel like that!' I said, raising my eyes to heaven.

'Poor little Mary!' Churen teased. 'Perhaps you should go straight back to your gorgio world.'

'Stop that!' Mary ordered, dressing her face in thunder clouds. 'I never loved you anyway, Churen Isaacs. You are what's called a holiday romance. Soon I will be back studying, and I won't even remember your name.'

'Ugh!' I said. 'How sad.'

'Forgotten so soon,' Churen agreed. 'All those nights and days that I shared with her, and they count as nothing.'

'I didn't *share* them!' Mary shouted, getting

bother-blue-face blotchy. 'I was asleep so they meant *nothing* to me!'

The moon shared Mary's sulks. It skulked behind the thickening clouds. The night grew heavy dark. The tall firs on the edge of Rollright Stones whispered a warning, before even they fell silent.

Strange sparky lights began to flicker from stone to stone, round and round, creeping ever higher like a hungry blue fire. We shared not a finger lick of excitement.

'OK, Great-gran, we've got the message!'

'The time for Churen to choose is now,' Great-gran's voice was thunderclap loud but midget-mouse scary.

'I thought the women chose,' Mary called up to Great-gran. 'I thought the women were the most powerful gypsies of all.'

Great-gran's face bellow-blossomed out from the clouds. 'Don't you know the saying, *The male of any species chases the female . . . until she catches him*? You should do, for it is the same the world over. If Freya has done her job properly, then Churen will make the right choice.'

'I have worked my best magic,' I told Great-gran,

'for you have taught me well. Dibby has walked full circle, both she and Briar have grown. Dibby is at ease in her heart at last.'

'But you have failed me,' Great-gran said crossly. 'Dibby is not whole. With Churen you could have healed, not wasted your time with silly love charms.'

'No, Ostrich! You are wrong, Dibby *is* whole! She is wholly Dibby, and everyone loves her just as she is.'

'But . . .'

'This time you are wrong!' I told my great-gran crossly, correcting her firmly for the very first time. 'Dibby *has* grown. She is deep-heart happy and needs no magic of mine.'

'No matter, it is done,' Great-gran said, and I was surprised at her calm. 'Take the handkerchief Churen holds for you. Tie the red knot that will one day make us the greatest choviar of all time.'

I felt rather than saw Churen leaning idly against the shimmering granites, clutching my not-too-neatly stitched handkerchiefs. His face was crinkled with laughter. His spirit seemed bubble-burst blithe as he waited.

'Oh, get it over with!' Mary said, not even vaguely

interested in the lapping lances of light that dressed the stones with colour. 'Take the noose that binds you for ever, and let me go home.'

Mary's mouth dropped as she suddenly pointed to the centre of the circle, where shafts of vibrating light focused. 'Do you see that! Can you see a black cat being made out of flames?'

'Offer the handkerchief, Churen!' Great-gran ordered. 'Offer it *now*.'

I closed my eyes. Churen and I danced, as moths round a candle, closer and closer we were drawn to the flames. Fire and water, earth and air, now or never. I let my insides tumble with joy until I could bear no more. It was the feel of fur that brought me to my senses. I opened my eyes. Pahn sat beside me, the touch of his fur bringing calm. 'The Rom must choose now.'

'Yes,' Great-gran agreed. 'It is time.'

Mary's face was box blank. Her fingers toyed with the acorn and sunflower necklace that I had given her to wear. They said clearly that she loved him, even though her tongue had lied.

'Do you think I have a mind of my own?' Churen asked me lightly.

209

I thought of the pictured mirror that shared his restless nights. 'Are any of us totally free?'

'Enough!' Great-gran ordered. 'Choose. Bastet will not stay for ever.'

'I choose Mary Jane Loveridge Reed.'

Mary's face went pasty pale. 'Why me?'

'I learned that I loved you,' Churen said, releasing his scarlet belt and letting the mounting winds weave it about them. 'Red hair, funny freckles, caring heart. Mary, you are always in my mind.'

'I have to finish school,' Mary said, suddenly nervous now the choice was hers. 'And I want to . . . and the cockerel said nine years . . .'

'Take the handkerchief, Mary, then you have all the time in the world.'

Mary needed no second bidding. She took the silks from Churen's hand. There was no bolt of lightning, no clap of thunder, no frantic calls of crowing cockerel. They just stood hand in hand among a riot of red ribbon as Bastet, goddess of joy, bound them tangle-tight happy before fading back into the flames.

I stood alone wearing my brightest smile.

'I'm so sorry, Freya,' Mary said, a spasm of pain masking her happiness.

'There is no need,' I said, anxious to see her joyful again. 'Be happy.'

I found myself stroking Pahn's sleek black fur and burying deep the pain in my heart.

'But . . .'

'But nothing! Have you not even noticed Great-gran is gone? She only really meddled to make sure I was strong, free to be what I am. She never really wanted to choose for me.'

'But . . .'

'I told you! There are no buts. Take Churen, he's yours.' I pushed Mary gently, to show we were still friends. She chuckled and pushed me back.

'Great-gran will rest easy now, for I need no man to share my dreams. I am the greatest choviar of all. You have been given Churen, but I have been given Pahn!'

A Little Gypsy History

Gypsies are a nomadic people. Their origins have become a little lost in the mists of time.

It is almost certain that the gypsy originated in India. They were most likely to have been a tent dwelling people of fairly low caste.

The word gypsy is actually a corruption of the word Egyptian, and one theory was that the gypsy may have originated in Little Egypt, which in itself is confusing, as this has been variously considered to be Egypt, Little Armenia and Epirus.

Gypsies are known as Arzigans or Athinganoi in Asia Minor. These names are derived from an Indian sub caste, with the meaning, 'Not to be touched'.

Many of them were said to earn their living by sorcery.

Romanes is predominately a spoken language, passed from mouth to mouth, in a travelling culture. The backbone of the Romany language is Indian, corrupted, or adapted, over the passage of time, with additions from countries such as Iran (Persia), Romania, Turkey, Hungary and, eventually, Western Europe.

For a people so widely travelled, it is surprising how constant the Romanes language is, despite regional variations. This is probably due more to dialect than evolution. The pure Romany gypsies that I have spoken to are extremely proud of still having a language that can be understood, no matter where they travel.

True Romanies remain a proud race with a very individual culture, which, even if not strictly adhered to today, is of great historic importance. Their greatest fear seems to be the intrusion into their lifestyle caused by the modern Traveller.

Romany gypsies have always considered themselves to be a race apart. I believe that they should be allowed to remain so. It would be a great loss to society if a culture that has existed so successfully for so long should be destroyed.

Romany words used

Athinganoi	a particular tribal caste
Bender	temporary canvas tent
Bowie-zoomi	snail soup
Buni Manridi	honey cake
Chavi(s)	girl(s)
Chavo	boy
Chíriko	bird
Choviar	witch
Didakai	half-Romany
Drúkkerébema	prophesy
Dukker	to tell fortunes
Festa	celebration
Gavver	policeman
Gorgio	non-gypsy
Hotchi-witchi	hedgehog
Juvel	Romany women

Kel the bosh	to play the violin
Kokko	uncle
Motto	drunk
Patteran	road sign
Poshrat	half-blood
Prala	brother
Rokker	talk
Rom	man
Romano chirickli	water wagtail
Sastra Pot	stew
Scry	search
Shoshi	rabbit
Vardo	gypsy wagon